OPEN ENDS

M. HOLZHAUSER-ALBERTI

D. W. MARTIN

ILLUSTRATIONS BY RON MILLER

DEDICATION

In gratitude to our high school English teachers, Ms. King, Lucas, and Newell, for every day that they put up with us.

"If you love life you also love the past, because it is the present as it has survived in memory." — Marguerite Yourcenar
Translation by David Downie

CONTENTS

1 HERCULES AND THE CLOAK OF INVISIBILITY

Part I

"Give me one good reason why I shouldn't just blow you away right here, right now. Just one, that's all I'm asking for," the big burly man said, as if it were a simple task any person alive could easily handle.

The big burly man pointed a steely, chrome-looking gun at the scared little man in the corner. Steel? Chrome? Whatever. It was a gun. You get the idea.

He got closer and closer to the scared little man, taunting him with the gun in his hand. The scared little man spoke nervously.

"Uh...you know Frank...I'm not exactly in a conducive environment here. I mean this isn't exactly a best practice for brainstorming...so...maybe if you'd just point that thing a *little* bit away from me.."

"YOUR LIFE DEPENDS ON IT HERCULES!" Frank shouted, then looked confused. "And by the way, I always wondered, is that your real name?" he asked.

The scared little man looked around his workshop and thought about it for a second. "I'll tell you the answer if you don't aim that at me anymore, Frank."

"OH FORGET IT, I don't care WHAT your name is! How's about this answer, how's about you tell me one bloody stinkin' reason why I should spare your miserable thing you call a 'life' and let you walk out of here on your own two feet instead of carried out by my two friends over there," he said, pointing fifteen feet away, where two other goons in suits were standing by awaiting orders.

"That's right Frank. We don't mind carrying him out, he looks like all of a buck-twenty," one of them volunteered in agreement.

Frank laughed his approval. "Yea, and that's about all his pathetic life is worth right about now, a buck-twenty!"

The two goons laughed, as if on cue.

"And I only have a dollar in my pocket Hercules. So tell me again, what was it you were supposed to convince me with as to a reason why you should continue to live another day?   Because it *certainly* wasn't those bullet proof bracelets you sold us, now was it?"

Hercules looked a bit surprised. "Why, what was wrong with the bracelets? I made them perfectly. I tested them and everything. They could easily stop bullets! Hell, they could stop a bazooka if you used them correctly!" His regained composure seemed to put Frank off balance, as if he couldn't understand why the little man wasn't afraid of his gun anymore.

"Well..." Frank started. "But, you told us they would work just like in the Wonder Woman series, and they didn't work like that, did they fellas?"

"No way boss," the goons answered. Frank continued.

"And so now, minus Bobby, who mistakenly because of YOU thought he was safe wearing them, we get to find out that they don't quite work the way you sold them to us, now do they Mr. Hercules! And speaking of Hercules, you're an awful tiny guy to be calling yourself Hercules, just my opinion though."

There was a moment of silence. Hercules seemed resigned in disappointment. He took off his glasses and wiped the sweat from his forehead with a rag from his pocket.

"I told you guys when I sold it to you," he said, "that in order for them to work like they do in the Wonder Woman show, you have to have lightning fast reflexes just like Wonder Woman. Now I'm guessing that Bobby didn't exactly have lightning reflexes right? I never said anything about how the bracelets would improve your ability to anticipate where the bullets would be coming in at, and to move your wrists to the appropriate juncture in space-time to deflect those incoming bullets. I merely stated, when I sold the product to you, that the bracelets had the same or better *stopping power* as the Wonder Woman bracelets, that's all. Nothing more than that. You can't just expect that I can build something that can do the impossible. You've got these unrealistic expectations of me, plain and simple.   It's not fair."

Frank was befuddled. He looked over at the goons. They shrugged their shoulders, not knowing what to do either. A lot of help they were, he thought.

"Well okay now listen," Frank stated assertively.   "That might explain the bracelets, but then *how* do you explain that so-called 'lasso of truth' you sold us that also didn't work? You know, the one where you rope them with it, and they're supposed to fess up to everything they know, just like in the Wonder Woman shows? A lot of good that one did! Remember boys? How before Bobby got shot, he lassoed one of them with the lasso of truth, but then they just cut through it with a pocket knife and shot him?"

"I remember boss, I was there," one of the goons agreed. "He had them squirming for a while, we were shouting questions at them to get them to answer, but then they just cut through it like it was confetti or somethin'".

"Confetti?" Hercules asked. "I don't think that's the right analogy. Confetti is pre-cut already."

"Right, that's what I'm saying, it was-"

"SHUT UP!" Frank shouted, regaining control of the situation. "The point is, we had them captured, just like in the Wonder Woman show, and we could have gotten the truth out of them. We could have gotten some very useful information. But then not only did THAT fail, but also those stupid bracelets that Bobby was wearing also failed! So what do you have to say for yourself, Mr. Overpriced Inventor who invents GARBAGE?! Because right now to be perfectly truthful with you, it ain't lookin' too good for you if you know what I'm saying."

Again, Hercules took a moment to stop and think. The sweat was dripping down his forehead, and it wasn't because of the temperature in his workshop.

"Look Frank, I'll tell you again. When I sold the lasso of truth to you, I made no guarantees about whether or not someone could cut through the thing with a pocket knife or any other utensil. I simply stated that it would have the effect of making the lasso-ee have to tell you everything truthfully. Can you prove to me that if they didn't cut through the rope, they wouldn't have told the truth? Because if not, then you really have no case."

That seemed to stump Big Frankie. Never before had he tangled with a man with such argumentative capability such as this one. But what if he *does* have a point, Frank thought to himself. I mean, what if those guys *hadn't* cut through the rope... would they have told us the truth then?

"And besides that," Hercules continued, "I just have to wonder what kind of men you're hiring who want to be just like Wonder Woman in the first place."

Frank snapped back out of his wonderment. Now the little man was making disparaging comments about his goons.

"Now you listen here little fella," he angrily began. "Don't you EVER talk disparagingly about the clowns I got working for me, you understand?"

Hercules could tell he was angry and he meant it. Best to lay off for now.

"Yes Frank, I understand. I'm sorry," he offered.

That seemed to calm him down, Hercules thought. Now what though? He still has that stupid gun pointed at me.

"You know what I'm gonna do Frank, just for you," Hercules said, which caused Frank's eyebrows to raise up in anticipation. He continued. "Just for you Frankie, because I like ya...you know, even if we have our disagreements every now and then...I'm going to give you – free of charge – my latest invention. I want you to be the first to try it out. Just for you Frank, because you're my best customer."

Frank looked over at the goons. He didn't want to appear to be caving in to Hercules once again. Yet he was excited about what the latest invention might be. And free of charge? Well that was like a birthday *and* Christmas all rolled together.

"That's right Frank, free of charge," Hercules repeated. He could tell Frank's resolve was melting away. "Now put the gun down and I'll show you, it's right over here."

Frank complied and seemed to take on the manner of a kid anticipating that mommy would soon be giving him a lollipop.

"Free of charge? Oh, what is it, you have to tell me! I can't wait to see it!" he said, lowering the gun and eager to try it out. "Is it the x-ray goggles? You've been promising me those for a long time now."

Hercules raised a hand and pointed a scholarly finger. "No, but you're getting warmer Frank."

"I am? Why, am I sweating or something?" he was confused again. "Oh! You mean I'm getting warmer with my guesses?"

"That's right Frank, you're getting closer to guessing what I have for you to try out – free of charge. It's right over here. I'll give you one more guess to figure it out before I show it to you."

That seemed to excite Frank way beyond what any adult would normally exhibit. "I'm closer huh? I'm really warm huh? Oh gosh, what could it BE?? Let me think now. It's not x-ray goggles..."

"No Frank, it's not x-ray goggles."

"And it's not...let's see...is it an x-ray helmet?"

"An x-ray helmet Frank?"

"Uh huh."

Hercules was never surprised by any dumb idea Frank came up with. "No, but good guess. It actually has nothing to do with x-rays. It's my latest, greatest masterpiece: The Cloak of Invisibility."

"NO WAY!!" Frank shouted, jumping up and down. "Like in the Lord of the Rings you mean??!!"

"That's right Frank, just like what Frodo himself wore. Here it is, try it out. It's just your size."

2 BLACK RAIN

"Tell me about it," she asked with genuine concern. The request took me by surprise. It was the first time anyone had asked me to recall something so near and personal to me. It made me think for a moment. How does one go about describing the loss of a dear loved one to a perfect stranger? Her request seemed a bit intrusive at first take. I was still in the recovery process myself and was in no position to begin a recollection of events that were previously best left forgotten. Or were they?

Perhaps this stranger had a better idea about the pain I was going through than even I myself had realized. It was as if this kind woman had known a thing or two about suffering in her life. Who was I to deny her some of the detail, when it seemed she so desperately needed to hear it even more than I needed to tell it. She was so nice, and quite frankly I was appreciative of the fact that even in a small town café where no one knew my name, someone still cared enough to take the time to talk to me.

I closed my eyes and conjured up an image of my beautiful wife. In the end I suppose – or at least hoped – that telling her some of my grief might also help heal the wound that had scarred my heart. Perhaps it could make the wound a little less deep than it was before.

I gave her a version of events that was very surface and glossed over. I have trouble conveying to other people the sheer enormity of suffering that I had been through. I've saved some of the more personal details for only you, the reader:

"Does it hurt?" asked Dr. Koppa, a grey-haired gentlemanly physician, whom I had easily imagined as coming from a long line of physicians dating from 18th century stock, by the manner in which he carried himself.

"No, it doesn't really hurt. But it is bothersome," my wife told the doctor. "When I talk, my ear pops. It's as if I've been swimming for hours and I get a lot of water into it."

"Oh my, your ear pops?"

I wasn't sure by the sound of his response whether he was genuinely alarmed or just playing the good doctor, taking his patient's every concern with the utmost seriousness. I knew that Dr. Koppa was among the best, trained in a highly respected private college in Chicago, with years of biology study and even more years of medical practice. I wouldn't have it any other way for her, regardless of the cost.

"Yes, it pops. I wake up and hear this black rain pouring over my ears. This dense black wall – liquid – filling my ear. I can't hear my children say hello to me in the morning. I can't hear my husband talk to me. He thinks that I'm handicapped and he no longer loves me as before, when I was strong. I can't hear myself breathe; it makes me crazy."

My heart sank when I heard those words. She hadn't realized that I was hearing every word she spoke from around the corner, behind a wall. I couldn't believe that she felt like I didn't love her as much. I felt more guilt at that single instant than I could in ten other lives. Her suffering voice made me abandon any right I ever felt to self-pity.

"How about coming to the office again next week?" the doctor asked. "If your ear's not hurting, then there's no emergency. How about Monday afternoon?"

Dr. Koppa spoke in a calm and reassuring voice. He went on to explain in medical terms about what some of the possibilities could be. But at this point, his diagnosis was uncertain. We would need to wait and see. Next week. Next Monday.

I sat staring at a black screen in front of me, one of the heart monitors at the station mere feet from where my wife and the doctor were softly speaking. How long had I been staring at it?

The possibilities of what felt like a wall of black rain filling the ear canal. The doctor's words were a bit difficult to make out, though I managed to hear some of them. Possible impact on the ear drum.

Possible adverse effect on the body's sense of balance. Needing to rule out any kind of mestasis or infection, though the chances of that were fairly remote at this stage. I wanted the doctor to speak up, to be more authoritative, a bit more directive, make bolder statements, and reassure his patient in that way.

"Monday at 5:30 then. Thank you. Goodbye." The split second during which I had captured my wife's plight in the other room was over. The doctor was saying good-bye to me and her, and we were leaving the office.

"Yes, I was a bit reassured after that office visit," I told the waitress in the café, as I waited for my friend. She had been standing there listening to my abbreviated version of events, keeping the carafe of coffee at bay. "But any reassurance about anything, let me tell you, has gone out the window. One second you're here and the next... I sometimes wonder if there is any hope for redemption on this earth. Mine seems to have left... disappeared into thin air, mingling with the black rain that had begun to destroy her ear. You know, it took her away from me within a year of that diagnosis. No hope for redemption left in this world."

I looked out the window of the café. It was a bright and beautiful morning. My friend would be here any minute.

"Well honey you just look out that window and you'll see all the beauty that's still left in this world. There's redemption, believe me. Your wife would want you to go on living wouldn't she? Now you just go out there and live."

3 LOOKING BACK

Looking back, it's not absolute proof of possessing great parenting skills, as my father ended up being the only one who spoke without noticing that I didn't talk at all. It's no proof at all. One would rather be convinced of the opposite. What a rotten parent! Over 20 years ago did the conversation take place, which I'm going to recall now, but the standards of modern parenting, which include a good deal of listening, really listening, to your children, and eventually to your spouse, easily reach back that far and even farther, encompassing the period of the early 80's and therefore the actions of my father. He would have no excuse if one were to accuse him today of bad parenting, and yet, how many individuals really are of their time? Even myself, with all the education I've had, living well into the 3rd millennium, I sometimes feel my values, my emotions, to be from the Dark Ages.

Anyway, the conversation took place. It's that which he wished above all, I believe now, that the conversation was had, that it occurred. I guess a real fault in parenting would have been to not have it. It took place as if it was determined to take place, take place by parental obligation, resembling a natural act, like a bowel movement, in which mental reflection, though present, is secondary, powerless in the face of larger governance, resigned to not changing such deep urges, nor change what is written.

On my part, the conversation was very much a passive act. If it had been possible, I would have liked to disappear that day, but I was only twelve years old. Twelve year olds cannot disappear just like that because family and friends will worry and call the police. Especially well-behaved twelve year olds like myself would cause immediate worry and reaction from family members. Anyway under no circumstance would I have thought about running away from home. I was much too scared of being by myself, of being out on my own. A simple white lie would have been welcome to permit missing the occasion, but a white lie, such as used by many an adult, didn't occur to me. My filial obligation was as strong as the one I presumed motivated my father.

How many times, now and during our conversation, did I wish to tell him that he was way off:

"*Papa? Total kalt. Du bist ganz weit davon entfernt.*"... that he wasn't getting warm at all, moving more and more away from the truth as if in a children's game. That he was way off in the end wasn't my fault.

It was a day in February, cold I remember; we wore long coats; he a dark blue one, cut fairly well, not too long, cut close to the body as was customary in the late 70's in Germany, clothes that weren't flashy, that government employees could wear, though he wasn't one of them. My father sold cars, owned a car dealership.

We were walking away from the car park and walked off to the right side of the newspaper building, passing the linen store, where my mother had bought linens over the years, some of which we took with us to the New World, never finding something as comfortable and as soft again. We were now heading along the train tracks, leaving behind us the small iron and wood "ox" bridge, named that way long ago because cattle would cross it on their way to the market where they were sold. Heading towards Bad Munster, the next town, a community of retired people enjoying the thermal baths for which the region was known for so long.

What were his first words? Something along the lines of him having heard that my mother and I would be leaving for Spain together.

What would have been the big deal anyway? My half sister Brunehilde lived in Spain and it would have been normal, under the circumstances of divorce, for my mother to try to regroup, consolidate, live with her children. Perhaps it was that all along which bothered him. Difficult to say, really. The events lie back over twenty-two years.

"I heard that your mother and you are going to move to Spain," said my father.

What was I supposed to say? He said it in order to have a response, but I didn't say anything. I tried not to lie. At least not so soon. So I didn't validate what he was saying because I couldn't. I think I said nothing because I had nothing planned since I hadn't expected what I learnt others later would refer to as a father-son talk, nor had I rehearsed any lie. My mother had told me that it should be known that we were leaving for Spain, and not for the U.S.   Mastrodom was in divorce proceedings with his wife, and it had to be kept secret that he was seeing my mother. Many years later I wonder why we had to say we're leaving at all.

"You know, your mother will probably meet another man, and you may become less important," he stated factually.

It was actually some real psychology coming from my dad, as if he had a vision or something.

"Really warm. *Heiss. Heiss.*" I was thinking to myself... "*Brulant.*" I'm thinking to myself. Mastrodom was already in the picture and I had accepted him in our lives by the time my dad spoke to me, but he was right to say it. Certainly he was closer to the truth than I granted him. Many years later I realize that he was trying to prepare me for growing up, warn me of a world where the interests of adults got in the way of growing up and growing old innocently. I was twelve at the time. One divorce was already behind me. One may wonder if I wasn't already very wise when I was having the conversation with my dad.

We were almost reaching the railway crossing and began to turn back. I was amazed at the length of our walk, of our talk. He had really taken his time and had thought things out; it was going to be our goodbye talk. I saw him once more after this conversation when he had discovered the truth and refused to speak to me any further. He said then that nobody lied to him like this, not even or especially not his son. With the lie I was excommunicated, no longer his son. He turned his back on me, robbing me and himself of a proper goodbye. He was probably relieved that he made of me the guilty one, he who left my mother in shambles.

We walked back, and it was my turn to ask him what he thought would happen to me if by chance I was to stay with him in Germany. Did he already know that he was going to die within a year? He ended up confirming my fears that I would end up going to an *internat*, a boarding school. My biggest fear popped up its head: to be abandoned, left alone in a boarding school. My lie was beyond hope of retrieval. His talk could lead to no good, at least not then, and yet when I think about it now, knowing that he tried to help me grow up, he was consistent. Others never see their dad; I at least knew mine, or rather got to know him until I was almost thirteen years old. I really didn't know him well then. The question I had asked him was oriented in a particular way since my mother had prompted me. Divorced parents, especially the one of two parents who gets left behind, the loser, do a lot of that: prompting their children. It's really bothersome, and yet they have to do it if only because they're adults and the child finds himself, without the proper arms or preparation, in an adult world into which they have been catapulted by the divorce. It's not really a fault of theirs that they intervene so much. Perhaps my mother remembered my fear of staying in a boarding school. I tend to believe that she used this information unconsciously and without vicious intent. Oh my, I ask myself now, where's the key to all this? Why this helping growing up coming from all sides all of a sudden. *Maudit divorce*! Why had he spent weeks away around the time of my birth? What had happened during the pregnancy? Why did I sing myself to sleep for years (always rocking to one side, consequently causing a deformation of my rib cage)? It's something children in foster centers do, abandoned children (though I heard my brother-in-law sang himself to sleep. Happy family, I would think.)

The walk was great; I wish I had been older to have spoken better with him, with that person he was on that day. Still a wish by a child from divorced parents? Always wanting to be older, wiser, capable of undoing the impossible, reversing the divorce and bringing the parents back together, return them to their old selves, the loving selves, where they loved each other and were content with their situation. Forty-five years old he was. After the divorce, I had always thought that he could not possibly be happy…Under what circumstances did he die? I know so very little.

4 POETIC JUSTICE

"Tonight, tonight, by the candlelight.
Tonight, my Love, I'll make you mine tonight."

Staring at the piece of paper in front of him with the words he had just penned, he gathered his next thoughts.

"What a stupid poem," he said, crumpling the paper and throwing it into the trash can.

He grabbed his trusty pen and began looking at a fresh new piece of paper in front of him, waiting for the inspiration to come. It had to come, if he just waited long enough. It was a near-inevitability. He could write anything on that empty piece of paper. He could write the next New York Times bestseller. Then it hit him.

"Tonight, oh yes tonight, my Love.
Tonight, tonight, you will be mine tonight."

He read over the lines a few times, waiting for the effect to soak in. "Oh my God, that's even worse than the first one," he sighed, crumpling up yet another piece of paper and making another basket into the trash can. The score was now Creepy Terrible Poems 14, Home Team 0.

Frustration was gaining on him like an evil villain in a swerving car chase, shooting wildly at 80 miles per hour from a rolled-down window. He thought he could tame it, putting a chain around his frustration and confining it to a few idle thoughts. But it could not be contained. He had to have her. He had to find a way to get her.

He turned the fan up on high because by now he was sweating profusely. Gallon upon gallon of empty water jugs lay around his feet, tossed onto the floor carelessly, a separate concern from his quest to write.   It was when he was most intensely concentrating on an unresolved matter that he seemed to get the hottest.

As his father had explained a long, long time ago, one should never give up hope, because hope will never give up on you. His real mother had died shortly after he had been born. Hope seemed vacated at that point and his father had wished he could have helped his poor wife, who lay dying of cancer at such a tender young age. But he could not do anything to help her. The best he could do was to tell his son "I tried". He would say "I tried, but I couldn't save that which I loved most dearly. Maybe this will someday be a lesson for you: don't ever fall in love unless you know for a fact that she will never leave you… and after all, how can one know that?" his father had said with a wry, melancholic smile.

He had his doubts about his father's advice, mainly because he wasn't sure if he could ever control his feelings, and because it seemed to him that his father had given up hope, just when he needed it most. Besides that, the idea that you could predict whether someone would ever leave you – and that you should base your feelings towards this person on a prediction – seemed ridiculous on the surface.

Perhaps his father believed that his son needed extra protection from the world, due to his mother's death, and the circumstances of his physical abnormality. The doctors had diagnosed the child with a rare genetic birth defect, which, as they explained to his father, had left him with heightened sensitivities to his surroundings; the extra-sensory ability coming at the expense of an increased metabolism. It was as if his body was acutely aware of its environment, yet at the same time required to draw in so much energy from its surroundings in order to compensate for this ability. As a child growing up, he was never really sure if it was a blessing or a curse.

He often felt like one of those superheroes he saw on TV. There wasn't a character with the powers of intuition that he had, but he was sure that if he wrote to the creators of the show, they would make one up just for him. His father had given him the nickname "Hercules" to make his son feel better about his illness.

His mind began to wander even further. It seemed like just a few short weeks ago that he had been sitting in the park, waiting for the girl that he was now infatuated with. If only his father knew now that he was pursuing a girl that he could never guarantee would stay with him, he would roll over in his grave. I'd pay to watch that, he thought.

"Why did you tell me that you wished I would just disappear!" he said aloud, catching himself, wondering how the thought became so urgent as to be uttered with his outside voice. He had often thought about it before, how on the last day that he saw his father, instead of receiving a fond farewell, he was left with only condemnation. The words left permanent scars in his mind. "So that's it? You're just going to leave me now, just go away and disappear somewhere? Well you know what, I wish you would just disappear," he remembered his father saying. He was only twelve years old at the time. Countless times he had wished with all his might that his father would take back those words... that they would visit again some day and his father would only have nice things to say. But they never saw each other again, and that visit – that second chance – had only taken place in his mind.

That chapter in his life had been written and the next one started, though the strains of influence from the previous stories were still evident. It was soon after he arrived in the new country that he began to feed his ravenous appetite for knowledge about physics and chemistry. He wanted to find a way to literally disappear. He never told anyone about *why* exactly that he was so passionately interested in absorbing all he could in each one of his classes. All of the other students and teachers just thought he was a natural born talent. But he had to try so hard. He had an inner fire that could not be put out until he gave it his all... and when was that exactly? He would never convince himself he had given it everything he could until the moment he had achieved it, accepting no less than to prove to his father that he should never have just wished him away like that. A father should have said something like "I wish you would stay here with me." His father, from wherever he was, would one day see that he should not have been so callous. The inner fire – the force that drove him to reject satisfaction and complacency – was fueled by none other than pain.

And now he was focused on covering up the pain. Claudia, for a while at least, had replaced invisibility as the object of his obsession. She was everywhere in his mind. Last week he wrote a poem about how he was burning up with passion for her. Yet Hercules knew the sad reality: I'm no damn writer. And I'm *especially* not a poet. Oh, he tried the poetry slams before, and he even submitted a few hastily written lines to his high school writing club. They laughed at everything he submitted. They called him an amateur. They said it would lower the value of their publication to accept any of his work.

But would *she* laugh at me? Would she rip out my heart and show it to me, laughing hysterically all the while? Hercules thought about it for a moment and realized that the question was not whether or not she would laugh: the question was really, does she even know that I exist? He began thinking about the ways that he could get her to notice him. His talents were obviously not in writing, but he *was* good at other things which might pique her interest.

He knew that he was good at building things. In fact, he had already patented several chemical formulas to induce changes of moods, perhaps she would be interested in that. He knew that certain people *did* value and notice him – the Department of Defense had contacted him about his truth formula. The sex industry nearly knocked down his door when he published his patent on the "5-minute model". He was wanted by the big players. He was important to them. He had the brains that they needed, and they let him know it.

But was he important to her? No, it seemed, he was a nobody.

"I will find a way, one way or another," he told himself. "Tonight, I will find a way to make her mine."

5 PESTERPUFF AND THE CONCRETE SLABS

My dear Sister!

Just a quick hello to let you know how we are doing. I guess I could give you a call; it would make things so much easier, so much more immediate, but the budget's tight at the moment. It's not really a problem of money, if I'm honest; it provides me rather with a decent excuse not to call more often, and obliges myself to sit down and write a letter. All in all, you'll probably chastise me as so often you did during our childhood in the Old World that my way of doing things couldn't be more convoluted.

Of course, sitting down to write isn't so easy. The New World typewriter doesn't work over here; the desk I'm working on is really sub-standard. As you know my work involves a lot of sitting in front of the computer; therefore, it's the last thing I want to do on the weekend, but where was I: I wanted to let you know how we were. And anyway, if it weren't for you, whom would I write all these silly things to?!

The last few days have been very busy: I've been building a concrete fence around our house! What a horrible thing to do, yet it seems that a great number of Old Worlders do this. It makes me think back once again, with a tear in my eye, to life in the New World: sprawling lawns, no barriers, at least not physical ones, at least that's what it looks like on the surface. In some ways I envy you, but it all sounds much worse than it really is. The new house…it's no use describing to you how big it is since the unit measurements will have no meaning to you. Let it suffice to say that we are surrounded from all sides. Not by enemies, but just other houses.   Luckily we get along just fine with our immediate neighbors and there hasn't been any declaration of war with anyone in the neighbourhood, immediate or extended.

Concrete fence…it's really a misnomer, but what do you expect from me, to be able to find the mot juste? I'm a connoisseur of rare books, my dear! You can't expect me to know anything for certain in my ripe old age (though I've always and will always be seven years younger than you!   Shh, I won't tell anyone your age; no one knows mine for certain other than Hildegard).   In Old World parlance one would refer to the low key, drab construction as poor man's stone fence.   Small rectangular concrete slabs slapped one onto the other with a good amount of mortar in between.   Oh, what lack of imagination, oh what lack of funds.   Do you now understand better? Certainly not.

Anyway, building this fence forced me out of the hearse, the house, sorry.   Pushed to the outer limits of the garden, don't imagine anything sprawling here, it's not prairie, I began building away when my neighbour, standing next to the entrance for I don't know how long, started talking to me:

"She's a beauty (I translate). The last real sedan that Ford built. I remember an all leather interior version, even the power window buttons were leather. It was dark blue, sold to a lawyer in Mainz back in the late 80's."

Mind you I knew vaguely what he was referring to since a couple of days earlier I bought our new used car in order to transport, amongst other things, the concrete slabs I've been telling you about. I guess I'm a little unfair translating the first sentence of his the way I did. He said it in a manner much less coarse than what I might have led you to think above. It was said with a genuine touch of nostalgia.

Just saying that word, putting onto paper, even saying it through the computer, virtually, makes me pause, makes me want to write down, fix, or fight in some ways, the great wave of nostalgia that overcame me this morning. Twenty years it has been. When my Scaulie language teacher threw away the pictures I had used to work on an assignment she had given us. I can't even blame her, as much as I would like, because she asked me at the end of the school year if I wanted them back. I had said No. There were extenuating circumstances. Of course, there were. There are always excuses. It was the end of the year. I was fourteen or so at the time. It was the time you left for summer vacation throwing away all your papers. Some of those pictures were priceless. Not that they were worth anything to anyone. They were just the only pictures of me when I was younger. The best pictures I had found to do a good job on the assignment. Is it self love? Perhaps. I could blame scrap-booking. Do you know what this is? Funny, it's a New World thing I think. And yet it's Hildegard who seems to be doing it every other evening, when she's not watching the European soccer league.

Scrapbooking. When I first talked about it to this Welsh neighbour of mine, he thought that my wife was into horse racing, or worse, making travel arrangements over the internet. It's not even that Hildegard's at fault. She didn't ask me for pictures of me of any kind. She was just sitting there in her leather chair doing a scrapbook and it made me think back, no it was much more violent than that, I was catapulted back decades, to this crucial moment, where I said No, and I'm the only one to blame..........

Where was I? The Car. It's an ugly car I tell you. It never existed in the New World, to the best of my knowledge. I actually bought it because it's so ugly; I thought it would discourage thieves.

"They don't make 'em like this any more." He was referring to the impeccable leather interior. It's true. The interior was in very good condition. Like new. Amazing for a car almost twenty years old. I told my neighbour that I got it for a very good price, and I was on the point of asking him to help with the concrete slabs when Hildegard came out to bring us some sandwiches. Oh, what a darling. WHAT A DARLING. It's the thought that counts. Not only did she prepare ham sandwiches which I don't eat, but she also brought them out only minutes after I got started working. It was too soon. I wasn't sweating yet. Not even a tiny bit. Well, anyway, this New World custom of bringing out sandwiches made my neighbour step inside the garden and grab a sandwich. Again, he didn't really grab it; I make it sound much coarser than in reality. He started eating it. I could have sworn that he had been on the point of denying me any help on his part because of the interior redecoration he was doing with his son and which was leaving his back in a sad state. Bastard. He then took a glass of milk. Oh, dear Hildegard. DEAREST HILDEGARD.

We were working away on the fence in the early afternoon when

Hildegard's sister drove by. She ended up saying hello to us, but made her way straight to my neighbor's neighbor's house. Not a smile, not a real hello how are you, no explanation. That was very much unlike Castanjeta. So we left the concrete slabs and followed her to her car whose trunk door stood open. We crept up to the trunk, looked in like grave thieves, but saw nothing. Castanjeta's trunk was a model of Old World order. But even that World Order was known to explode once every so often. What it had contained was tucked under Castanjeta's arm while she was heading towards the flower beds.

In the flower bed pointing towards the West she posed the remains of Claudia, her twelve year old Cocker Spaniel who, I presume, had succumbed to a final episode of grand mal seizuring. My neighbour went off on an explanation of how his neighbour kept a pet cemetery, how it wasn't legal in these parts, but how thoughtful it was of her anyway. I wasn't able to cry. Even seeing Castanjeta in relative despair couldn't warm me up to crying. She didn't cry either, but you could see she was shaken up (Thank God, she hadn't had a car accident). Were we too much Old World people not to cry at such an occasion? Would you have? Writing about Claudia's death makes me wonder. Do you think that we have become jaded by years of living with our father? He who performed three to five autopsies per week for twenty-five years of professional service.

I wasn't able to have a look at Claudia as Castanjeta had already closed the shoe box on her, it serving as a casket. If I had seen hers, my reaction may have been even more jaded, banal, nothing out of the ordinary. Father never much talked about his job, his profession, even with me. What would there have been to say? What would it have explained about our upbringing? Or about Mom's suicide?

Old as stone and I finish this letter with a number of questions, the same questions as before, that resist answer.

I didn't tell you. We expect visitors. My daughter and family will be staying with us for a couple of days. We'll see our new grandson, Pickles, the 5th one, I think; I start to lose count. I hope I won't be losing sleep with this one!

Take care. With all my ever enduring love, Pesterpuff

6 PAUL

Paul: What happens if it doesn't work in the North? What's your plan B?

Yuna: I'll ask you in marriage, but you're not obliged to answer in the affirmative.

Paul: I'm not interested in that. You'll give me a picture of your head and your body and I'll put that on ebay.

30 minutes later...

Yuna: I have to go North because my Mother's not well. I'll be back next week.

Yuna was looking for a job up North for over 3 years, Paul thought. He grew pensive as he wondered if she had been serious about the marriage offer or not. If his friend John were here, he would tell him that women never joke about marriage. Why didn't he just ask her if she was serious or not? What prevented him from asking her? Write a question, instead of making that somewhat demeaning statement, he thought in retrospect.

Ah, women, you can't live with them, you can't live without 'em. Twenty years he had been in a relationship with Yuna, until 3 years ago when things came to a head and he had left home. Ever since, he was running around like a chicken without a head. He was putting on weight, and he hated himself for the lack of making a sound effort to turn things around physically.

He was a proud man, he thought. It was okay to have answered this way, he was saying to himself, because he was not to be taken for a Plan B. Did she even listen to him when he spoke? He sometimes got the impression that she didn't care at all about his daily life, his problems at work, there were plenty of those lately, his feelings, his whole person really. She never asked how he was doing; it was always only about the kids. She loved to point out to him that the kids were only sick when they were with her and how come it was like that? Because he didn't do what was necessary so that in the winter months they'd wear clothes thick enough to protect them from the cold weather. How come they ended up at a point where they didn't even listen to each other?   He didn't know why there were so many questions and so few answers at the same time.   He listened to her, every time. This respect for the other person, he had learned that from his parents; it was part of the parental education he had received as a young immigrant child growing up in France.   Not only was it important to listen to your parents, but you'd be damned if you didn't listen to your older brothers and sisters. Yuna had become part of this family, as if she were a blood relative of his.

Where had they gone wrong? It wasn't in bed; there everything was just fine, as they used to say to each other. Just fine, with a smile on their lips burning bright with a flush of excitation, like a much deserved cigarette. However, the moments of satisfaction didn't last very long, and, before they knew it, they were back to arguing. After the split-up, what was left of his love for her, went into taking care of their two boys, who spent most of their time with him, though the family court had decided on a 50/50 arrangement.

One week later
Yuna: I'm back; my Mother's feeling better. She sends her love.
Paul: Is she ready to marry someone, too?

15 minutes later...
Yuna: She's still grieving her husband, Paul.
Paul: If you're still grieving me, how come you'd be willing to ask me in marriage?
Yuna: Oh, that? That was only a joke. You took that seriously?
Paul: ...yes, I did, after thinking about it.
Yuna: And, after thinking about it, would your answer be affirmative or?
Paul: I don't know; I didn't get that far.

Yuna: Ah, men, can't live with them, can't live without 'em. That's why we love you.

7 COLUMBO – THE EARLY YEARS
GOODBYE, LOVER; GOODBYE, MY FRIEND

As I'm nearing the retirement age, I find myself contemplating human nature more than ever before. My own memory seems to be still in very good shape; no signs of letting down, not like some other vital bodily functions. Curious by the way that the brain seems to be letting down so little as the rest of the body falters.

My editor had proposed to me the idea of working on some early material. I don't know why all of a sudden this seemed to be more interesting than the more contemporary stuff I was doing. Perhaps he saw a buck in it, and that sufficed to go ahead with the idea. Works for me! Retirement's expensive.

Human nature's such a curious thing to investigate. Every investigation I've ever led has had to do with it. So, where to find material for those early years? I remember an event many, many years ago that had such a profound impact on my memory, though the impact was purely materialistic; it had nothing to do with amnesia or any other impact on those little grey cells. It's not an event with grave consequences. Simply my French language teacher threw away the best pictures of my youth which I had used for an assignment. Everything that I had retained as being idealistic about my youth still existed somewhere in the recesses of my mind, but the proofs had vanished in one single swipe. It's like hitting the wrong button on the computer keyboard. Again, I find something to be curious: a single simple gesture could have such grave consequences on the development of any story from those early years that might be deemed worthwhile telling.

But those early years wouldn't prove to be useful other than provide the bucolic setting of an uneventful, happy childhood. So what to do? Some women are known to engage in an activity that keeps them and their loved ones quiet for hours. They engage in this activity with the kind of abandon that others pursue in passionate play or obsessively elusive goals. Scrapbooking. If you haven't heard about this pastime, then you have been living on another planet. But let me explain, for the purposes of situating the genesis of my first story, what it actually is and what it isn't. It doesn't have anything to do with booking bets, for example, as our uncles used to practice during the prohibition in sparely-equipped, half-lit, cigarette-embalmed back rooms. It also doesn't have anything to do with 90% of the activities that pretend to the title. Scrapbooking uses scraps of information. Ticket stubs, pieces of cloth, colored paper, bits of advertisement to come up with a collage, with a whole that is more than the sum of its parts. It's not glossy, but it is colorful. It's not perfectly centered photos, but those that weren't put on the mantel piece or sent to cousins. In the end, my first story is nothing but an exercise in scrapbooking. The perfect pictures being gone, I relied on what was left.

Ninety-eight note-card sized pages with a single message printed on them, a pad of note cards with a brown blotch scotched to the side; it didn't mean much and yet it represented my first real case even though I hadn't been an investigator yet. I don't know why I still had the pad. Was I waiting for the opportunity to finally tell the story? Was it pride that let me hold on to it because, not only did I know what the pad represented, but having retrieved it, I had potentially saved ninety-eight lives?

My first case takes us back to the mid-50's. I was barely 20 years old, but old enough to have moved away from home. I already lived in California at the time, but my freelance budding journalist job took me all over the country. When the job wasn't responsible for taking me to far away places, I took it upon myself to put some distance between my new home which didn't mean that much to me yet and where I would go. In the spring of 1954, I was just finished with an assignment in Oregon, covering gold mining, I went to Florida. One of my friends from university had accepted a lucrative administrative position on the decision-making board of the University of Florida. The place I stayed at was an extension of the main campus which at the time was in Grafton, a wonderful campus located on beachfront facing the Gulf of Mexico. I arrived on a Friday morning, not long before lunchtime. You must remember that we're in the 50's and that things were very different back then. All the little period details are crucial, not only in understanding the rest of the investigation, but in lending some added legitimacy to a story that in the end could not produce itself today.

What was so different back then? Oh, in the end, not that much. For example, when you passed a pretty woman while leaving a building, you still turned your head, to get a second innocent glimpse of her because you could have held open the door for her, to get a whiff of her perfume, etc. If you don't do this nowadays, you're really missing something. To get to Florida, I had to take the train. There was nothing like Amtrak back then. Trains were usually on time. Of course, the railway system was rather complicated back then and for parts of my journey I had to use my Army pass boarding non-passenger trains in order to be able to cut across the country in a reasonable way and gain some time. Perhaps I already developed my famous trench coat style back then because when I was in the train I kept clothing details to a minimum, most of the time just keeping on my trench coat without at night changing into a pajama. I guess my behavior could have been described as impulsive back then. The decision to visit my friend taking up a new job across the country was not premeditated, nor was he a particularly close friend. In order to bring some balance to my impulsive nature, I kept other things in my life especially stable; my clothes, my eating habits (I was a vegetarian long before it became fashionable), relations with my family (I had the habit of spending 3 weeks with my family between Hanukah and Christmas to the point where my family and friends were happy to see me leave). So there it is, part of the charm of telling the story of those early years, the secret of my trench coat: keep it simple and keep it clean. The trench coat I wore showed heavy signs of a night spent on a bunk bed in a coal train going from Arkansas to Florida. The train was empty, the coal having been delivered in some remote lake region where a microclimate was responsible for long winters. Fortunately none of the coal dust had made it onto my coat. If there was any smoke that had found its way into my clothes, it would have been difficult to spot (sniff?) because at the time I was still smoking cigarillos imported from the Old World, which in turn had imported the tobacco leaves from the New World. They kept me enveloped in what you could say was an invisible smoke cloud, reminiscent of the illegal booking back room atmosphere of the past. That I haven't developed a cancer 50 years later is probably due to the fact that I'm a vegetarian.

I had arrived at the main administrative building around eleven in the morning, giving me enough time to get oriented for meeting up with my friend for lunch. That was another different thing back then. You actually prepared going out for lunch and took time afterward to digest your food. We ended up eating together in some restaurant not too far off and exchanged a number of superficial comments with the sole consequence that I only remember him coming off as a snob in a fine suit which he had bought with his new salary. I forgave him for not asking me anything about my new life in California because he generally seemed happy, judging from the quantity of pleasant smiles he was sending my way throughout lunch, that I had made the trip all the way to Florida to see him. All those smiles and vacuous comments, they weren't even real exchanges of information, let alone anything else, made me regret coming, so I imagined to myself that I had come to test the mild climate in this part of the New World. I accompanied him back to his office and was on my way out. I headed through the front doors that were among the first to open towards the outside, a new ordinance stipulated that public doors had to open onto the outside, and not inwards, when I saw three or four other students heading in. The place must have just opened up after lunch (this is another thing about the 50's; QuikTrip and the like didn't exist; people closed shop during lunch; I guess you could say the 50's very much resemble some Old World customs that are still alive today). The 50's saw the traditional student body evolving; amongst the students that crossed my path as I was heading out were a number of women, African and Asian-Americans.

One woman struck my eye. She was the last one in the group of students making their way into the building. One could say that she dragged a little bit behind. She seemed to walk more slowly as well. When she brushed by me, I got a glimpse of her; short dark red hair, a violet dress that stopped at her knees, and a poise that made me want to capture her fleeting image. I regretted being so old in comparison and wished that I in turn had not rushed out like the others had rushed in, which would have allowed me to keep the door open for her. Her poise was underlined by an expression so singular that it still haunts me today.

The vacuous conversation I had with my friend actually got me started believing that I had come all the way to Florida to see the coast line. I was heading out, just walking aimlessly, almost forgetting that I had asked directions to the nearest beach. The lady at the front desk had given me directions to this wonderfully romantic spot, she said, which would be very quiet at this time of the school calendar year. It was about 15h00 when I arrived in a small bay area that was free from cheap hotels and any other commercial venue. The quietness of the gulf almost left me thinking that we were next to a lake, that time had stopped, that cars were non-existent. I began to slowly let the scenery set in and was close to agreeing whole-heartedly with the front desk lady that this place was truly romantic. The coast line could be described as rugged, but very low, as you might find in parts of Ireland. Certainly in no way did it make you think of a traditional Florida coast line as you might find on the Eastern side of the State at about this time of the year or a little later. There was no hint of Palm trees, but rather a deserted half-prairie which gave way to stony islands and then low tide. The smell wasn't salty. All this made me think of the California coast line in part at least: Monterey Bay, the home of John Steinbeck. He was my hero back then, as was the case for about half of my class in journalism school. The faintly orange sky was attracting me and I kept walking forward, my shoes starting to get wet. The smell of the algae was beginning to get overbearing and I stopped in my tracks, realizing that it was late and that I had to make it to the hotel to get my bags ready.

The taxi set me in front of the hotel and I went up to my room. I had a good two hours to get ready and thought that a quick nap would allow me to be less edgy when it came to not sleeping on the train. I was heading out on another coal train shortly before midnight. The phone rang. It was still early in the evening, the sun had not set yet; it was my friend. He wanted me to come back to campus as a new development had occurred which he wanted to consult me on. He didn't say anything else. I agreed and headed back to campus in another taxi. About fifteen minutes had elapsed between me hanging up the phone and being next to my friend, completely changed, the two of us standing with a police officer in the stainless steel campus cafeteria.

"She's difficult to identify in her state, but I'm positive. Helena Stark. A wonderful human being. Such a bright student. I don't know what to do Peter." He spoke in shopped off sentences and didn't look at me.

The police officer stood to the side, and I wasn't able to figure out if he wanted to get on with business, whatever that would be, or if he was bored.

"There's no blood," Karamba went on saying. "No blood anywhere. She's been exsanguinated. There's a trail of blood all the way down to Lovers' Grove." Lovers' Grove, that's the name of the wonderfully romantic spot I had been to this afternoon. There's been a murder, and I was the prime suspect.

It took several minutes to understand that Karamba had not called upon me because I was the prime suspect. Rather, because of my journalistic talents, he thought it worthwhile to have someone there, a scribe, to record the events as they were unfolding. Campus police did not exist at that time, and the local police force was represented in full by the currently present member, Head of Operations, and local sheriff, all in one. Perhaps you're beginning to understand, or at least guess, that what we saw in front of us, an utterly disgusting scene of murdered flesh, was the reason why this story has never made it. The 50's were a quiet time. Such a scene simply didn't fit in.

"Come a little closer, Peter. I want to show you something."

I didn't know what it was to communicate. Her innards spread over her and covered her body, they seemed to quell up, hide the rest of her body. Her face was barely visible. Her eyes were closed. Thank Heaven. The dark red hair had lost its luster. It was the girl I had seen just hours before walking past me. I rushed off to a corner of the room and vomited.

The police officer, Brandy was his name, gave me a verbal account of the finding. Nineteen year old female, enrolled in medicine, found dead in the cafeteria at 17h30, curious finding, no rigor mortis yet setting in. In turn, I found it to be curious to make it such an essential finding of the investigation, if there was one, of her hanging limply on her chairs. I made a note of it to find out later why this finding was of importance. He continued.

"She seems to have had a date at Lovers' Grove mid to late afternoon. The killing, if I may say so, (nobody prevented him from saying anything of that sort), seems to have taken place there. The murderer, her lover perhaps, seems to have cut her throat in a way as one might cut the throat of a pig. She lost all her blood on the way from Lovers' Grove to the cafeteria. How she had access to the cafeteria off hours is still under investigation (I was wondering hard who else was on the case!). She seems to have suffered minimally. I assume she was tranquilized just before the killing. (How he knew all those things was beyond me, but he said it with such an authoritative tone that I believed him, taking each word as if it were the word of truth, and making note of his way of going about the investigation.)"

"No coitus seems to have taken place; the rubber's clean. No sperm in her vagina or elsewhere, from what we can tell," said Brandy.

"What do you think, Columbo?" said Karamba.

I walked around the body twice before responding to him. "Grotesque" that's the only words I could find. To this day, I had not been able to describe what actually had been in front of me. Getting different angles of the body, I glimpsed a little note card stapled to her dress hem. I bent down to read it. Nothing. Nothing was written there. No splotches of blood even. "Not a crime of passion, a premeditated murder I would say, but I'm no expert."

"What should I do? I'm getting together her files and will have to give her parents a call right away. Chief Officer Brandy's going to write down the findings, I suppose, and continue on with the investigation. This is really terrible. I'll have to get in touch with my hierarchy, though most everyone will be out of town by now."

He seemed to retract into his own world of administrative issues and general complicatedness. Brandy had left the room to take in the information that was coming through in his car. Just random tidbits of information. Nothing seemed to be related to the case at hand. By that time I was dizzy, both in my head and my stomach. Karamba had called in the paramedics to clean up things. Brandy took some pictures and sat in his car, making out the report. What had he already seen in his lifetime that left him so uninterested, so even tempered? It was both a strength and a weakness not to be able to identify with the most cruel of circumstances. And yet he struck me as conscientious, as professional beyond his years, and in some ways it was this Chief Officer Brandy who represented an entire police department in this area of the gulf coast that sowed the seeds for my own interests for changing métiers, leaving behind journalism and making it one day to inspectorship. He wrote and wrote like I had not seen anyone capable of before and yet I had worked in a number of fine publishing houses and newspapers where gifted writers abounded.

I left the crime scene that evening, barely asking him if it was alright for me to leave. Karamba had walked back to his office and was busy telephoning half the state. Of course, the murder was important, but did it merit such a trahlahlah from him? I couldn't help but be disgusted with his behavior, however professional it was in retrospect.

I left town, as scheduled, on the 23h54 coal train leaving for Arkansas. Coal trains left during the night because they traveled in a coal dust cloud most of their way due to the lack of proper riveting. Coal investors found it more acceptable to the public to do their dirty business of sending coal half-way across the country at night when the coal clouds could not be noticed by passers-by. I couldn't sleep, haunted by the images. And yet I was sure that I would never be able to write down what had happened. Things change. Times change. And I find myself able to write today thanks to the little souvenir that the murderer left me ever so inadvertently.

Still dizzy, as if in a dream, I got up and walked down the aisle. Exceptionally I had been placed near train manager quarters, the reasons for which I was not entirely sure of. The train driver room was in the first wagon which was separated from mine by a dead space of about 25 inches. I took a long hard breath. It was good to breathe some fresh air. I could not notice if there was a coal cloud or not, but in any case the cold air woke me up a little.

8 PANACHE

Part I

"Alright class, now if you remember correctly from our last session, we had a discussion around 'what are the five key elements of a successfully engaging story'. Does everybody remember that?" He paused a brief moment for a response, still facing the whiteboard. "And they were what again, class? What was the first key element with which to grip your audience," he asked hopefully.

"Exciting intro," someone said from somewhere.

"Ah yes! Exciting intro! Glad you brought that up. That's our first rule." He confidently changed colors of dry erase markers, pulled the cap off, and wrote '1. Exciting Intro' on the whiteboard. "The well-written story will have an exciting intro," he continued.

"Dr. Pesterpuff I have a question about that," one of the students interrupted.

"A question! Oh yes, yes of course, I just love questions! Go ahead Mark."

"Well... how exciting does it have to be? I mean, do you always know when it's exciting? Because what's exciting for you may not be exciting for me."

"Hmm, imagine that," Dr. Pesterpuff replied. "Well that's an interesting question Mark. The answer is that it must be exciting enough to the average person on the street. If you can get the average person on the street to pick up your trade paperback that you've just written, glance at the back cover, and find themselves overly titillated by its premise... and then perhaps they read the first few sentences of your first chapter and they say to themselves 'I simply MUST purchase this trade paperback!' then you've got yourself an exciting intro. The well-written story will lure the reader like an unsuspecting fish. Alright then? Good. Okay so what was our second rule for creating a 'successfully engaging story' class?"

"It was the 'Journey from Innocence into Danger'," the amorphous blob sitting in the classroom said.

"Fabulous! Yes that's correct, the 'Journey from Innocence into Danger'. Yes, every good story has got to have this element in it, in some fashion or another. Very good. Okay that was #2, our second rule of the five key elements. So far we have 'Exciting Intro' and 'Journey from Innocence into Danger'. And what was our third key element then?"

"It was 'Bad, Bad People'," someone mentioned.

"Correct, 'Bad, Bad People' is right," Pesterpuff replied, writing it on the board under the first two rules. "Every good story must have very bad, bad people arrayed against our innocent little protagonist. Very good then. Alright, next? Our fourth key element?"

"'Pressure to act'," a girl volunteered.

"Very good Nikki, pressure to act. I can tell you paid attention during our last tutoring session," Pesterpuff winked and smiled. He wrote 'Pressure to Act' under the first three rules on the whiteboard. "Now remember, this 'pressure to act' should be at the end of every chapter as well, so as to compel the reader to continue turning those pages for hours on end in order to induce a sense of apathy about the time of day. And definitely, 'pressure to act' at the climax of the story – this is what adds the element of edginess to your work. The well-written story will have edginess. And finally, what was the fifth of our five key rules for a successfully engaging story?"

"Panache!" the whole class said in unison.

"Panache! Yes, that's correct class!" Pesterpuff squealed in delight and did a little dance. "Now you remember, 'Panache' is that certain.. 'je ne sais quoi'. It is that element of a good story that makes it unique to the reader... that makes it stand out in such a memorable way and gives it a higher degree of class and sophistication than it would otherwise have had. Remember this class: the well-written story will have a certain amount of flair, a certain panache. We don't just do, as the French would say, 'metro, boulot, dodo'. We generously spice it up."

Dr. Pesterpuff put the cap back on his dry erase marker. "Alright excellent, so there we have it, all five of our rules. Please be sure that you have these memorized and can repeat them back to me on the spur of a moment, as I may call upon any of you at any time during our discourse. Or, if I see you at the shopping mall for example, I may say to you 'Hey you, the 5 rules, what are they? Recite them now please' and then you'll be expected to repeat them back to me without so much as skipping a beat. Everyone got that? Good. Now let's move on shall we? If you remember from last class I asked you all to write a little 'teaser' script. This would be something that you would find on the back of a novel that gets the reader interested in what your story is about and makes them want to lay out their hard-earned cash for what you've produced. Every well-written book will have a teaser script on the back cover. Alright then, so who would like to go first?"

Mark raised his hand. He was sitting next to the amorphous blob, who couldn't raise anything.

"Excellent Mark! Just stand right up here in front of the class. Give us the title of your work first if you would please, and then read your teaser script to us."

Mark got up in front of the class. He cleared his throat and nervously spoke.

"65 Million Year Wait. Um, that's the title," he said, laughing nervously, seeming to wait for Dr. Pesterpuff's approval.

"Excellent! Go on Mark. I certainly can't wait 65 million years to hear about it."

Mark continued. "Okay then. 65 Million Year Wait. 'Oh my God! One of them has escaped!' 'What are you talking about Dr. Schmeckles? What do you mean?' 'One of the dinosaurs has escaped!' 'Oh my God, you're fired!' The dinosaurs had waited 65 million years for their chance to eat us. It was supposed to be the other way around. Scientists were finally able to recreate all of the dinosaurs. The UN decided to raise the dinosaurs as a food source in a world of ever worsening drought. But something went terribly awry, and now the dinosaurs were on the loose, forcing us back into caves." Mark raised his head, finishing his teaser script.

"Bravo, bravo!" Pesterpuff clapped, encouraging the rest of the students to clap as well. "But one thing Mark, and that is… well, you know, 'Panache'. Yours doesn't seem to have enough of it, quite frankly. It just doesn't want to grab me in a uniquely sophisticated kind of way. Panache, Mark, Panache! Flair! Fashion! Style! Vogue! But other than that, there was the 'Exciting intro', you've got that covered.. 'Oh my God! They've escaped!' Love that. I also love the title, '65 million year wait'. It's like 'come on guys, hurry up and clone us so we can eat you, we've been waiting 65 million years!'" Pesterpuff giggled. He was weird.

He continued his critique. "You've got the journey from innocence, trying to create a food source in a drought. You've got bad, bad people – or in this case, dinosaurs it seems. However, you seem to be missing the 'pressure to act'. Or, I suppose, it's before everyone gets eaten, I don't know. Maybe you have it in there. But bottomline Mark, my advice to you: Panache-it-up! You know, throw in a little more panache here and there. Apply liberally. You know, it's funny, it reminds me of those recipes that call for just a 'hint' of garlic. To Hell with that! I say throw in the whole clove! Panache, Mark, Panche! Got it?"

Mark nodded and took his seat.

"Alright then," Pesterpuff continued breathlessly. "Who is next?"

Nikki raised her hand excitedly.

"Excellent Nikki, please stand up and read us your teaser script, title first please."

Nikki was hot, Pesterpuff thought to himself. So very young and sweet. Probably melt in your mouth like butter.

Nikki opened up her notes. "The Night I Kissed Simon LeBon," she read, then looked up. "I'm hoping this will become a Broadway musical someday!" She spoke excitedly, shaking the whole upper portion of her body as her enthusiasm bubbled over.

"Well one never knows, Nikki, it could happen. Please read your script for us then."

"Okay," she smiled and continued. "The night I kissed Simon LeBon. 'Come on dame, you know I'm a wild boy!' Simon was persistent backstage after the concert. It was a wild night at Madison Square Garden in 1984. Way before the Wedding Album, way before Pop Trash. 'I'm hungry like a wolf for you baby!' Simon was an animal. He wanted me so bad. Yet I was a Catholic school girl who had taken a vow of chastity. Call it good fortune that my parents had named me Rio, because here I found myself backstage after the concert, the #1 groupie at last. 'Is she dallying with me now? Please, please tell me now Rio, because I can't hold back the rain' Simon pleaded. Here was my chance to kiss Simon LeBon! If I didn't do it now, I may never get this chance again! Oh, what was a devout Catholic school girl like me to do? What a dilemma! And yet I closed my eyes and saw Jesus drawing near for a kiss. It was then that I knew what I must do, for Jesus wanted me to."

She closed her notes and looked at the ground for dramatic effect.

"Excellent, Excellent!" Pesterpuff stood and clapped. He demanded a standing ovation from everyone else. "Nikki if there is one thing I have to say about your script it is this: Panache! Your story is just oozing with it! What style! What flair! What fashion! What vogue! Great work Nikki, you are up and coming!"

She smiled broadly and took her seat. Pesterpuff seemed to calm down a bit and caught his breath. "Well alright then, who is next? Who in their right mind thinks they could possibly top that? Now class, this will be our final script reading for the hour. We have other topics to go over besides this. We'll get to the rest of you during our next session. So who would like to go next then?"

A boy raised his hand.

"Alright, very well then," the teacher agreed. "Let's see what you have to follow Nikki's hot, hot script."

The boy went up to the front of the class. He took a piece of paper out of his pocket and carefully unfolded it. As if this were his moment to shine, he proudly began:

"My Cloak of Invisibility."

Part II

Dearest sister,

   This letter may come as a surprise to you. I know it has been such a long time since I wrote you last. I was in my garden yesterday, planting the tulips. Tulip-planting time, as they say in the colloquial. This year's planting season had come a bit too early for my liking. However, who was I to argue or make a fuss. I was genuinely pleased just to have an excuse to get out of the house, even if only for a few hours. Hildegard's scrapbooking by this time has become an obsession. She has invaded the walls of our living room with scraps pasted here and there, turning our home into a living page turner! Oh how I do fear she will one day come at me from behind with a giant roll of tape and plaster me to our bedroom ceiling, just to look at me each night and remember me fondly. Oh dear, what thoughts I have! I have become consumed with this constant fear of someone trying to get me in one way or another. That's why I love the view from the garden so much. With the concrete fence securing us quite nicely, I have but little to worry about whilst wiling the day away out in the garden.
   So you can see why I love to spend hours and hours out there, away from the "world" as they so euphemistically refer to it. If I had my druthers about it, this thing they call the "world" would instead be called a "pile of poo." Poo is all that it amounts to these days. Well they can have their poo as far as I'm concerned. The only poo I need anymore is the stuff I'm fertilizing the tulips with. And boy oh boy, did I spread it on thick this time!
   Oh it's not going to be like last year, believe me. Last season's bulbs were a bit on the malnourished side if you ask me. They didn't glow like they were supposed to. You know dearest sister, people have come to expect my bulbs to be the brightest! Well that woman Frances down the road has been spreading something on her flowers that made them better than mine last year. Her tulips were lush and radiant, like the glow of a nuclear meltdown. That's about how I felt about them. They were far, far prettier than mine, but such tragedy! Well she got the best of me and I wouldn't be surprised to find out it's because she's been spreading dead animal ashes on them. She is truly sick and

perverted, and I must warn you dear sister, if one day you read on the news about her going missing... well, some things are better left unspoken!

You remember how I told you about Castanjeta going over there with her dead dog? I'm telling you that woman Frances is evil. She was gunning for me sister. Last year was the first time I was outscored at the annual tulip festival. This year is payback though, I'll make that b eat her tulips, courtesy of a little secret ingredient of my own. I'm telling you, I'm going to lay it on thick. No, it's not the manure I told you about before. I thought for sure Frances was going to have her way with me again this year. And then I met this wonderful man...

He didn't tell me his name but I saw him sitting in the park one day while I was out and about. He looked like a real loner. I said hi my name is Pesterpuff and I offered him some friendly banter about the weather and how lovely the birds were singing, attempting to ascertain his sanity level... perhaps he was one of those escapees from the asylum Hildegard and I had been hearing so much about lately. Well crazy or not, he seemed friendly enough and we got to chatting away. He seemed melancholic in a way, I couldn't quite place it. It was as if he was feeling a pain of longing. Yet he refused to tell me why. So anyway the subject got around to how lovely the flowers looked this time of year and of course that was my opportunity to seize control and dominate the conversation with my wonderful knowledge of tulips and flowers, etc. I couldn't tell if he was truly interested in what I had to say or if his mechanical head nodding was just another way of burning extra calories on some trendy new diet plan. Oh these diets, sis, who can keep up! Hilly and I just eat whatever comes our way.. oh now, that did sound horrible! Oh dear, if she saw what I am writing you, that would be the end of it!

So long story short, this man in the park whips out this ornament full of gray powdery substance.. it looked like dirty powdered sugar to me. He asked me to taste it, to make sure it was genuine. I wasn't even sure what it was supposed to be or how my tasting it could possibly confirm its authenticity, so I politely declined. Then he told me the most amazing thing: he assured me that a little sprinkle of this powder over my garden would make the most amazing, biggest, and brightest tulips I had ever seen!

I was flabbergasted. It was too good to be true! Here sitting right in front of my eyes was this man and his wonderful powder – just the ticket I needed to beat out Frances once and for all. I ended up paying nothing for it! He just handed it to me and then went about on his way. He said he just remembered something he had forgotten and had to hurry along. I really didn't care, because I had in my hands the secret ingredient that was going to make Frances lick my boots with that old, tired tongue of hers. No more humiliation. Those days were over. Frances, I'm coming to get you!

R. Miller

Well sister so there I was, back home in my garden that afternoon. I sprinkled some of the precious powder over my tulips. Then, still holding the ornament in my hands, my curiosity got the better of me – you know me too well! Carefully – looking around to make sure no one was watching – I stuck a wet finger inside. I pulled it out and tasted it. It was magical and sweet. I began to feel an oncoming surge of euphoria as the thought of regaining the crown ("Tulip King!") began to overtake me.

I was laughing giddily, sprinkling the contents over my precious tulips. I tasted the powder again. Delicious! Wonderful! What had I been missing all these many years? I could kick myself. I actually tried to kick myself, but fell over laughing hysterically. I began making snow angels in the dirt, even though there was no snow. Why must it only be in snow, I thought. So confining. Who makes up these rules anyway. The thought of someone making up these stupid rules made me laugh uncontrollably. I thought I was going to die. Oh sis, you should have been there. Words cannot do justice to how incredibly funny it was.

I opened my eyes as my laughter subsided. There were little garden gnomes dancing all around me. They were the cutest little fellas. They were dressed up like Alpine villagers, and were skipping gaily around me. I could hear their tiny laughter, as if coming from little microphones dancing and skipping around me. Some of them were busily chatting with each other and seemed not to notice me. Others were looking at me and smiling, as if in admiration. They all seemed so very friendly. I thought to myself that if they should become hostile, I could probably wipe out most of them before they could climb onto me and start biting. But they were not hostile at all. There was nothing but kindness, glee, mirth, and all those other gnome-like characteristics.

"What are you, some sort of little faeries?" I asked one of the older ones. He appeared to be in charge, watching over the others, yet was taken aback by my question. He smiled confidently, yet spoke with a hint of indignation.

"No, we are not *faeries*. Do we look like *faeries* to you?" He made a wide sweeping gesture with his arms... or at least, as wide as you can get at 6 inches tall.

I looked around and saw not a single wing on any of them. Perhaps I had pissed the little guy off. He spoke again.

"We are the garden gnomes of Tulipville. My people have lived here for centuries. The magical powder you spread over our land has freed us from our shackles."

All of the little gnomes nodded in agreement as they continued their celebration.

"You have freed us from the wrath of an evil witch who has kept our people enslaved for over a thousand years."

"Is her name Frances?" I asked.

"No, not Frances. Her name is –" and he let out a piercing screech that hurt my eardrums. He apologized.

"Sorry, there is no direct translation of her name into your language."

"Let's just call her Evil Bitch."

"Works for me."

I don't know how they did it, but these little fellas just kept dancing gaily around and around and around with carefree mirth.

I found myself becoming slightly agitated.

"So, like... do I get a reward or anything for freeing you little freaks from a thousand years of brutal oppression?" I asked. I figured it was worth a shot.

The little guy's face lit up.

"Yes, of course! Whatever you want. It can be anything. We will grant you your wish."

Well of course I already knew *exactly* what I wanted. They said 20 foot tall tulips should be no problem at all.

Well, I end for now. Yours ever so enduringly, pesterpuff

9 TIME STEPS

Part I

I haven't slept for three days.

It's funny how you stop noticing things the way you used to, like you've become numb to them. You don't notice the chill air. You don't notice the sun shining directly on you, or reflecting off the ripples in the lake. You don't care about these kinds of things. When the love of your life has passed away, you don't care about much. You just know that you feel this incredible, overwhelming void. It is a void that nothing can ever fill.

How can I enjoy the sun, after all, when you are not able to enjoy it? How can I keep track of what I have eaten... how can I eat at all, when you are not here to share it with me? It's a missed meal perhaps... a hunger pain in my stomach, but what is it really, besides an insignificant human wish. Compared to the eternity of absence I feel without you here, it means nothing.

There's a flower that has bloomed at my feet as I sit here on this park bench. I've been coming to this park and sitting on this bench for such a long time, and yet I don't remember a flower ever coming into bloom in this patch of grass. It was years ago that I first came here. This was where I met you... do you remember?

Thoughts that I once considered absurd, such as this flower being a sign from you that you are okay, I now readily entertain. In my desperate and dark condition I feel ready to accept any kind of light from you. But only from you. I won't fool myself with false hope. If it is to be a sign from you then I should surely recognize it. You would not leave it ambiguous, open to interpretation. I plead with you, or whoever is taking care of you now, to not let it be such. It is cruel enough that I will go on living. I never would have said this to anyone publicly, but at this moment I feel fragile beyond repair.

If I slip into that void with you, would it be wrong? What should tie me to this world, when all that I want from all that exists… is to be with you. I can't pretend that my will is always strong enough to overcome this desire. And yet the silliest notion just might save me: your little poodle Anjolie. She is mine to take care of now. She is all that I have left of you anymore. I know it sounds whimsical, but she is still a creature that is full of life. You once took care of her, and now… I must do the same.

But the pull to join you is so very strong and it keeps bringing me back here. Am I only pretending that I have a reason to go on existing in this world, when you are not here with me? I just might stay… if only to take care of Anjolie, whom you loved so very much. But I remember how you would always say that in life, you have to play the hand you're dealt. Well this seems like such an awful hand. These cards don't seem anything like fair. And yet, you would say, "play it". I know you would say that. Even from the other side, I can hear you saying it.

I don't want this loneliness. I'll take any form of distraction. I beg to be interrupted. Any manner of diversion from this awful empty pit I feel in my stomach right now. Words cannot describe the feeling of absolute black emptiness. My God, how I miss my wife.

But alas, I am probably at the wrong place for such an offering of distraction. A park is such a peaceful place, a place more suited for quietness and solitude… perfect for privacy between you and I.

So I sit here on this park bench where we first met, and can you believe, I am holding you once more. Nothing like the beauty you once had of course, for all that is left of your physical body is now ash. Here in this urn, I still hold you. It's pathetic I know, but it's the only thing I have right now. It's impossible to hold you in any other way.

And now the time has come. Where these flowers grow up at my feet, I will spread your ashes. I can't think of a better way to celebrate your life then to return your beauty to this earth. The cancer that struck you down has not defeated us. You will return to the earth and bring forth new life. I believe this flower is a sign from you that you wish to be spread amongst these things of beauty. It is only fitting for you, nothing less could do.

I will open this urn and spread your ashes, my love, just as soon as this odd looking man leaves the area. He seems to be approaching me. Well now isn't this something. Here I was, finally prepared to bid our final adieu in this solemn act, and now it appears as if our farewell will be interrupted by this doddering old fool. He's striking up a conversation with me. Something about birds and flowers. Something about panache. I am just nodding my head in agreement. Oh god. Please go away you pestering dunderhead. But smile and ignore him as I might, my love, it's obvious that he's not going away. Now he's asking nosy questions about what's in the ornament. Is this the sign I was looking for?

"Oh this? Yes, it is quite a magical looking ornament isn't it. But what's even more magical is what's inside of it." You must be intending for me to give this man your ashes? I shall comply with your wishes.

"It has very special properties and should only be used for making the flowers grow," I tell him, and he seems very excited about the prospects of doing just such a thing. I hand him the urn and say a quick prayer. He's too caught up with the new gift to even notice me saying goodbye. Oh, how I'd like to disappear from this reality for a long, long time and never come back until I'm good and ready.

Part II

Dear Diary,

I had a nice day in the park. And some thoughts came to me as I was walking on my way home. It's my first time writing to you in a couple of years. However, recent events have forced me out of this cocoon I have grown accustomed to, and you might even say, have come to enjoy. And now this story – this metamorphosis – must be told...

I wish it were not so. Ever since you passed, dear Julia, my life has been nothing but a blur. Pointless. Meaningless... life itself has continued on, though seemingly without me in it. Heck, even my work has suffered. And I don't have to tell you – as you know me all too well – that has never happened. My work always come first, my wife second.

What I am about to tell you is hard to believe, even for me.

Looking back, it all seems like a very vivid dream of sorts.. the kind where when you wake up you aren't even sure what is real and what isn't. It's as if the memory itself is only but a dream. Perhaps it is true what they say: life is "but". And as we row, row, row our boats, I have to ask... to what end?

It shall be our secret that when I was younger I had the ability to affect the physical objects around me: couches could be set ablaze, people made to feel uncomfortable.. merely by suggestive thoughts. My mind was an overworked engine, output manifested in various effects on the environment... what some would call "paranormal"; others simply "mysterious" or "curious". And yet, the reason for these strange anomalies has forever eluded our joint quest for truth. That is, until now...

You see, I've stumbled upon a dark secret which even the most brilliant minds in science have seemingly overlooked. Yet it was right in front of their faces the whole time, and there is every evidence to believe that what I've found in my laboratory work – and meticulously validated through intricate, hundreds-step long proofs – is completely, and totally, 100%... Truth.

I must tell you this in the strictest of confidence, for the truth is indeed stranger than fiction, and I am guessing indigestible for most, as even the most stalwart advocate for scientific supremacy will surely be somewhat surprised by these findings. My dearest friend, you must promise me this: you must promise not to tell a soul. Consider it as though your very life would depend on it, for if my feeling is correct, it just might. I don't have to tell you who "they" are, as I am sure you are quite aware, but I must tell you they have been following me again, and it has not gone unnoticed. I suspect the reason is obvious.

We, as theoretical physicists, have always known that in order for the forces of nature to be united at the elementary beginning of existence, a theory of convergence – of "everything" - must exist. We know this to be true, for both the quantum and relative forces were as one in the beginning. The infinitely large was at one time infinitely small. And so as a natural course of events, the infinitely large can be derived mathematically from the infinitely small, in the sense that planets behave as atoms, galaxies as molecules, and so on.

And yet, of the eleven dimensions postulated to explain a theory of convergence, you know as well as I that only four of the eleven are known, and the other seven remain hidden. And the universe turns about on its axis and continues to exist, even though we are only familiar with and able to explain a mere five percent of its contents, the rest lost to so-called "dark matter" and "dark energy". But it is only dark to the men in the hats who have increasingly begun following me again, as I alluded to above. They are searching for the answer – WHICH I HAVE FOUND – building upon the work we completed while you were still in the familiar dimensions. Allow me to explain.

In so doing, let me just say it wasn't always this way. I was inspired to find the answer when listening to a song by Duran Duran, a beautiful little gem called "Starting to Remember". There was a certain lyric, "you've got to believe, time will heal". And for some reason it took me back to a memory – I started to remember, if you will – of a time when Jimmy Connors was interviewing the band. At a certain point during the interview Jimmy got up and demonstrated his world-renowned two-handed backhand, to which Nick replied that it was truly a thing of beauty, with a gliding form reminiscent of a sequence of notes played on his synthesizer, to which Jimmy responded with an offhand crude remark that doesn't bear repeating. Well the whole point is that the interview then lurched into a discussion surrounding rumors of disappearances and of scandals involving invisibility, to which Simon said something to the effect of, "Well, why should we be confined to dallying only with the visible world?"

And THAT was the serendipitous stroke of genius that immediately stirred me on to continue our quest! Why, in fact, must objects remain entangled only to the visible world, when we know that quantum entanglement exists, and that anything is theoretically possible at any point in time? And time being one of the dimensions, seven unknown dimensions, and space itself not a vacuum but a quantum field abuzz with an endless energetic sea of virtual particles. What is to stop objects that we see, feel and touch from becoming quantumly-entangled with objects possessing attributes of space and energy that we cannot see, feel and touch? And that was when I knew that you were still out there, and that you still exist!

Oh, the joy I felt, knowing with certainty you are still watching over me! You cannot imagine the relief. And I am not about to compare it to any sort of bowel movement, so please don't go there. It was literally as if the hopeful, sunlit energy of youth had come rushing back into my veins. I began feverishly working to resolve the mathematical equations necessary to prove this theory of everything. It took me *days* and gallons and gallons of jugs of water. And just as I was about to publish my theory, which I called "Dark Entanglement"... in a very reputable scientific journal mind you... well wouldn't you know it, but none other than *Duran Duran* just so happened to release a new album with the *same name*? And then they went on tour.

I was livid. I began to suspect the part of my theory about our thoughts existing in the hidden dimensions was true, and that somehow Simon LeBon had stolen my ideas. Well, let me tell you, if they were looking for bad karma they were certainly messing with the right dude. I wasted no time setting about on a very complicated plan to ruin Duran Duran once and for all. No longer would there be albums ripping off my work, or anyone else's work for that matter, contractual agreements be damned. I was going to make that band disappear. Like, forever.

Funny, I never told a single soul about this very complicated plan, and yet today I find myself being followed on what has become a near-daily basis by a man who is only pretending to be careful, ensuring we make eye contact, if but for a brief second. His appearance is out of place and time, as if he came straight off the set of an old detective film, complete with fedora and a dark, sooty trench coat that has not seen the inside of a laundry machine for years. The way he shows up at just the right time... entirely possible he is not of this dimension... thoughts may have become q-e.. well Diary, all for now... Herc

10 QUALITY

There's something to be said for a product performing the way you would expect it to, every time. I like quality – it's important to me. A product should feel a certain way, and do what it is supposed to do, and do it well. For example, my fedora feels like silk in my hands. It looks like cream. The firmness of the brim tells me it will be there for a long time, like a good friend, keeping the sunlight off my face, and the glance of my eyes out of view from passers-by. Quality is important to me. It has to work right, every time.

The precision of the Swiss timekeeping pieces has always fascinated me; the parts machined perfectly, each one in lock synch with the other. The attention to detail evident in my bomb building mannerisms was inspired, you might say, by the very diligent Swiss clock masters. I've always believed that without a model to emulate, one might never excel at anything. Case in point: as a matter of routine I transform boring bits of materials into precisely crafted explosive devices. Oh, it's not always that easy. Give me a few drinks and I might admit to a failure or two. I won't go into all the details, but let's just say my record's been marred by the occasional maiming. Those which render substandard effects are a shameful mark and cause me to do a lot of introspection about what could possibly have gone wrong. I suppose it's true that perfection is a goal always to be strived for, but never to be reached. I'm not so insane as to think that 100% of them will be winners. That would be unrealistic and depressing, in light of the facts.

It takes a rare bird to understand what it is that I've set out to accomplish. They never fully appreciated my obsession with this kind of detail back at the university. I could never convince those pointy-headed elitists that I was anything more than a dreamer. Chalk it up to their maddening ignorance, scoffing at my ideas about creating high quality products that could harness laws seen only at the very edges of physics. The saving grace in this little detour is that there are fewer of them scoffing now… and not because they've seen that my products really do work. It goes back to the discussion about the precision of Swiss timekeeping pieces. Those fortunate enough to witness my work firsthand usually don't live to tell about it.

Usually.

As I mentioned before, there was the occasional exception, one of them involving a professor of physics at the university who seemed to make it his divine mission in life to ridicule my ideas. He was a lot like the others, this Professor Stark, hung up on his tenure. Because I hadn't tenured yet, he and the rest would pour heaps of condescending scorn down upon me, as if they were watching the mushrooms grow. Unfortunately for me, the tidy little package with his name on it managed only to blow off his right arm and blind him in his left eye. He was fitted with a prosthesis and a patch over his eye and now runs around looking like Captain Hook. I hear he has two daughters living in the Tampa area, not far from an old friend of mine. It angers me to no extent that he should be so privileged as to have a family, when I was never fortunate enough to have one. But for everything in life that's not fair, there are ways of making them fair. It's what I do best. When you're born with a natural talent it's a shame to see it go to waste.

There is of course a dark side to having so much talent. It's not all good news. The downside is that I find myself endlessly obsessing – for hours on end without interruption – about ways to improve upon the quality of my work. It extends from even the simplest things all the way to the grandiose. The coffee cups that burst into flames after contact with a person's lips, for example. I still can't get the primary direction of flare to ignite exactly where I want it to: which is to say, in the eyes. Sure, it sets them on fire; burns their hair up like Michael Jackson and leaves them without eyebrows, but still leaves them with far too much time to react. The lethality of the flame is a strong concern I have. I've lost who knows how many hours of sleep over it, worrying that the product as it exists right now will only leave permanent scarring on the face. You might say I'm my own worst critic, but that's honestly not a sign of high quality in my judgment. And please don't tell me about that idiot private investigator, because I already know that he would beg to differ. His partner has a new face, but it's nothing I'm proud of. I wonder what ever happened to that Sherlock Holmes wanna-be anyway?

I know what you're thinking: small details such as the direction of flare are in fact just that, small details. I would leave it as a minor annoyance if it weren't for the fact that this obsessive yearning for quality extends to my greatest accomplishment of them all, the cloak of invisibility. Let's go back to what I said about being my own worst critic. Some might say that it works "just fine". It envelops the entire body in transparency. Yet I notice all the little details, and there are too many of them exposed for me to call this product "just fine". Beads of sweat, for example, may appear on the ground where the wearer stands. Somehow these drops of moisture manage to escape the effects of the cloak; whether because of problems with reflecting the water or the salt, I'm not sure. I haven't figured it all out yet and this is what I mean by the downside of talent: you never quite seem to get reality to match expectations. Call it counter-intuitive but I believe first in quality, and then in effect. A botched job done magnificently is to me far more preferable than a desired outcome achieved through some crude fashion. It's a shame that no one else seems to get it. My customers only see the parts that don't work. That's all they ever complain about. They hardly ever compliment my products for what they truly are: masterpieces that have overcome the supposed "rules" of physics.

My life is like a nearly empty gallery, and all the world is my canvass. What I paint, how I choose to paint it, and what I fill the gallery with are entirely up to me. That's the incredibly liberating and rewarding feeling I enjoy so often in this profession. It keeps me going. In a world of cruelty and injustice, I stay focused on the task at hand: righting some of the wrongs in this world. If I didn't do it, I'm not sure who else can or would.

10 DISAPPEAR INTO YOURSELF

"Why don't you sit down and have some tea, detective? You look so nervous, all your pacing around. Into the light, into the mirror."

"Do you know anything about the disappearance of that girl, Hercules? Come on, we're good friends here. You must know something," Columbo squinted, searching for a change in Hercules' face, any kind of a hint at knowledge.

"Well why do you ask me, Lieutenant? I mean, I think you already know the answer. You, of all people, should know. Into the light, into the mirror."

The missing girl. She was only 19 years old. Last seen telling a friend goodbye before going off to class that day. Her first week of college. She was spellbound by just the thought – the very idea – of going to college. Her friends said she looked forward to it so much because everyone had told her it would be the best years of her life. All the friends she would make. The things she would learn. The places she would go. But this Dr. Seuss novel turned tragic one day. She disappeared and no one's seen her since. I can't go an hour without her parents calling the hotline. The dispatchers just tell them the usual. I don't allow them to give any new updates unless there's a big break. Not my style to make promises I can't keep.

"You've been awful quiet, detective. Is there something wrong? Into the light, into the mirror."

"What's with that thing you keep saying anyway? You know," Columbo went on, "that 'into the light and mirror' thing you keep saying, what is that, some kind of Gregorian chant?"

Hercules had been polishing a mirror, but stopped for a moment. "Is this part of the investigation, detective?"

"No, it's just weird. Why do you keep saying it?"

"My my my, aren't we nosy today Lieutenant. One big nosy little investigation we have going on here isn't it. I mean, it's not enough to simply jump to conclusions about missing girls, no no no. Now one must disrupt a man's work with even more imposing questions."

"Okay, so explain to me how I'm jumping to conclusions by asking you questions about a missing girl?"

"I think we already know the answer to that Columbo."

"We? No, we don't already know the answer to that."

"Don't insult my intelligence, detective!" Hercules snapped. "You know just as well as I that we all have certain needs that must be met. And they're not always looked upon favorably by society. But when you see a girl as beautiful as this girl you're describing well... well, one can't help but become motivated into shall we say 'unusual' action."

Columbo saw his opening. "So because she was beautiful she had to die?"

Hercules laughed again. "Well detective, that's why they pay you the big bucks isn't it, to figure all that stuff out. Into the light, into the mirror. And to answer your question, have you ever thought about what it would be like to stare into the light of God? When I see the light of god, I see the face of God. I know you won't understand."

"No, I can't say that I am familiar with the light of God. At least, not underneath my lamp shade. Not that I wear lamp shades."

"I'm not talking about lamp shades, Lieutenant. I'm talking about the pure energy that is light, that is God. I know you won't understand today detective, but you'll understand someday, trust me. Into the light, into the mirror."

He continued polishing and providing only metaphors. It was as if he was polishing his own ego.

"And what about the mirror," Columbo asked. "what does the mirror have to do with anything? Is that God's mirror?"

"God's mirror. Hmmm, well that's an interesting way to put it. I hadn't thought of it that way, but I give you points for trying. No, you see, the mirror... well, this particular mirror in front of me here... is an instrument of perfection. The finest mirror that has ever existed." He smiled proudly. "The mirror is a fascinating subject. Did you know that Archimedes used a series of mirrors, whose collective power was sufficient enough to set fire to Roman ships? Did you also know that those made by the Venetians back in the 17th century are nearly priceless today?"

"No, I didn't know that, although my wife has very expensive taste in antique furniture."

"I see."

"You know what," Columbo said, looking for another angle, "I think I will have some of that tea."

"Excellent choice detective. Tea is a wonderful lubricant for the mind. Opens up all the channels of creativity in a way that nothing else can."

Columbo wasn't sure he was comfortable with that entire description. At least, not the lubricant part. He was miles away from any backup and he wasn't sure where this conversation was going.

"You know, on second thought, I just remembered my doctor's orders. I remember now he specifically said 'no tea'. I'll take a raincheck."

"Oh how tragic," Hercules said, polishing again. "Anyway as I was saying about the mirrors. This one you see before you is the finest ever produced in history. You could strap this baby up on the space shuttle and use it to lense faraway galaxies with unprecedented precision. The ones they use up there now are shit, like trying to read a book through milk bottle glasses."

"Well that is fascinating," Columbo said, deciding to try provoking Hercules into telling more information about the girl. "I really hope someday NASA decides to put your mirror up on one of their missions. That would do the whole world a big favor. You would be a hero."

He began walking towards the door. Hercules was eyeing him, unwilling to become a participant in what was to him an obvious attempt to manipulate.

"Yes because that's all I've ever wanted to do detective. Do the world a big favor."

But you're not dead yet, Columbo thought.

"But you see, detective, doing the world a big favor isn't something that can just be done overnight. Rome wasn't built in a day after all."

"Rome wasn't built in a day, and neither was your mirror, I take it."

"That's right Lieutenant, now you're catching on."

"Tell me something," Columbo said, moving in for checkmate. "Why were you so friendly with the girl in the park before she disappeared? You know the one I'm talking about."

"Don't try to pin me down with your little questions."

There was a silence. A silence which had no sound (unlike Simon & Garfunkel). Hercules looked like a man who had buried a crime scene in his mind and had convinced himself that he never saw it to begin with.

"Do you remember a poem by Robert Frost," Hercules asked, "about an unfished purpose: 'The woods are lovely, dark and deep. But I have promises to keep. And miles to go before I sleep. And miles to go before I sleep.'"

"I think *I* need some sleep," Columbo said, pulling up the collar on his coat, seeing that this was going nowhere. "Well I really must be going now. Thank you for your time."

"Oh you're most welcome Lieutenant. And be careful out there – that light you see at the end of the tunnel... could be a train."

"I'll keep that in mind," Columbo said, finally turning his gaze away from the mirror and walking out the door.

12 THE RUBBER TREE SESSIONS

Rolling Stone caught up with Duran Duran the morning after one of their sold-out shows taking place in Mid-America. Four of the original band members were present for the interview, Andy Taylor the lead guitarist joining in at the end. Here are some excerpts from the interview which turned out to be an unexpected jam session. Not bad from a band that was destined for pop oblivion.

Reporter: So what has happened since the Astronaut album, the making of the Astronaut album, and now the new songs?

John: (Pause)...*Giggle*...I don't know. (Simon breaks into a low, drawn out grunt and Nick hits the synthesizer; he literally hits it and out comes a number of strong base sounds. Duran Duran has started to play the new single of their Rubber Tree Sessions album, Bacteria.)

A little later...

Nick: The Rubber Tree Sessions stem from a need to make a very personal message. When we visited Africa last year in a humanitarian effort to improve living conditions for children in Zimbabwe, we noticed that the local rubber tree cultivation chapter provided a large part of the economical base for the country. We discussed it amongst ourselves and contacted Capitol, who agreed that it would be possible to donate 15 percent of all record proceeds to improve the livelihood of the rubber tree cultivation chapter. Musically, the Rubber Tree Sessions have brought us back to the early days when Duran Duran started out in small clubs in and around Liverpool.

Reporter: Duran Duran seems to have developed some soul in recent years, looking back to their own personal stuff to build upon, to go further.

Nick: Yes, that's right. We never thought we'd still be together after 25 years of being in a group…

Roger (interrupts): Well, most of those 25 years we weren't really together unless I missed something while tending to my farm!

Note from the editor (NFTE): The whole band laughs.

Nick: The early years were tough on us physically: Lots of booze, the whole rock and roll life. We enjoyed it, but it left us exhausted, drained of our creative energy. As Roger said, we drifted apart, pursuing individual dreams, sometimes without much conviction, without much vision. Duran Duran became a smaller group, and it became difficult to produce albums that people wanted to listen to.

John: My drug addiction became very difficult to master on a daily basis. We were touring half of the globe playing in front of ever smaller crowds of fans. The two were indirectly proportional: As the crowds were getting smaller, my need for cocaine became more oppressive.

Simon: It's really the Vendee sessions when we played in front of our friends, those that we could still call our friends, that things came together again after so many years. We were together to celebrate New Year's and Nick asked me if I still knew the lyrics to Rio (NFTE: Rio came off the 1982 album of the same name. Also remembered for its great video) Of course, I still knew them. And there we went singing away after so many years, not thinking about tomorrow…

Roger: Boy, did we not think about tomorrow all right! I ended up forgetting to feed my cows in the morning.

John: We ended up playing for over six hours. No stop. Many of the old songs came back as if they had never left. Some of the more obscure ones like Tiger Tiger or Secret October were fun to play again. Rio we ended up playing a dozen or so times: Each time with a different colour, with slightly different arrangements. I also played some lead guitar.

Simon: We were playing in France, in the Vendee. Some of our recordings over the years have taken us to France, but we had never been in the Vendee. We had absolutely no intention to record, but found ourselves in a friend's house with a full collection of amplifiers and instruments. It was sheer heaven. Except for your cows, Roger!

NFTE: At this time Andy came into the room. He seems to be stumbling in, looking for his sunglasses.

Andy: Oh, here you are. (NFTE: Andy was referring to his sunglasses). Now, that's better. I can think now!

NFTE: Andy has prescription sun glasses and without them he sees next to nothing.

Nick: With the Rubber Tree Sessions, we're experimenting with some highly classified military cloaking technology. It allows us to disappear at times during the songs, giving the audience the impression that the instruments hover on stage and play by themselves. Giorgio Armani, with whom we are collaborating on our stage costumes, gave us the idea and told us he had the capability to incorporate the new technology.

Simon: The invisible band. It's kind of the story of our life. Works out great back stage too when you want to see the little girls going to the bathroom!

NFTE: No one laughs. This band has come a long way since Girls on Film, their first big single. At one point this band was known as DD, sounded like the name of some amateur dancer in a Denver strip joint. The interview ended here.

13 LOVELY RITA

My Dearest Rita,

I suppose it is quite possible you'll have no idea what to make of this letter. It wouldn't surprise me: it's not as if you're surrounded by the romantic types such as myself! No, on the contrary, real men like me are few and far between these days...Meanwhile a woman's deepest fantasies go unfulfilled. Such are the sad state of affairs of our time. I have no doubt you'll find this letter a refreshing change to your humdrum and routine existence.

While I may not be a knight in shining armor, I may yet be the one who takes you away from all of this drudgy dreariness. After all, how exciting could life be when you're forced to stand behind a pharmacist's cage all day, doling out pills to nearly-dead decrepits? Was this a field that you volunteered to get into? Or were you pressured to do so by someone else – your parents perhaps? No matter. I really don't judge you for what you do, because the radiance of your beauty far exceeds the limitations placed upon you by the role of dutiful pill-pusher. I knew from the moment I saw you that day in the store some two years ago that you were "the one".

It happened quite by serendipity: I was only there to find some over the counter throat lozenges to soothe a wicked cough that had been getting the better of me. But what I found... was something I didn't even realize I needed until I was in your presence! I found you and immediately knew I needed you.

It may come as no surprise to you then that I've been keeping a watchful eye on you ever since then, my lovely Rita. What better to behold than your essence all this time? My eyes have thanked me for such charity, and you may think this is crazy but I feel as if my eyesight has actually improved! It's as if my eyes actually WANT to open up and behold the world again! For this, I have you to thank. And how could I ever repay you?

I thought perhaps I would sneak up on you after one of your morning jogs and thank you, but was afraid it may come across a bit too rash. Believe me, I'm no unrefined dolt, and I would certainly hate to frighten you or your dog Missy by suddenly appearing on the scene. So I suppose my little "thank you" will just have to wait for the right moment...?

It's funny Rita, but I feel as if we are old friends. I know so much about you and spend so much time near you, it's like you've become a part of me now... do you feel the same way I do? I hope so. I've seen you look around the way you do as if to say "I know you're out there watching over me like a guardian angel". It is very gratifying to me when you do this. It is what keeps me going and gets me out of bed in the morning. Think about this: it would be easy just to give up and let you face the harsh world on your own, but I was never raised to be so cruel. My mother taught me that when you find the right woman, you do everything in your power to hang onto her, rest her soul.

Well, this is a beautiful lesson, but what good is theory without practice? Do you remember the day you were fumbling around with some pills and that JACKASS "Richard" came up to you and asked "what do you say we go out for dinner sometime?" (!!!) You seemed flush, and I knew that you said you'd love to only because you felt pressured by him. He was an insensitive oaf, and you are better off without him around. Mother would be proud of me... remember when they recently found his severed head behind the bowling alley on 4th street? That was the one time that I've seen you act strangely: you didn't go to work for 2 whole days. It was very unlike you. I know you have a stronger work ethic than that, and to this day I am confused about it. What was going on in your mind? If only you would open up and talk to me. I am here to listen. Just say what you are feeling. I keep a very open mind and I would not judge you for something like that.

Alas, happier days have returned, and tomorrow will be upon us in the turn of a planet. Each night before I lay down to sleep I thank the stars above for placing our orbits in such close proximity.

All the Best,
Jack

ps. The new Duran Duran album is due out in May! (tentatively titled "The Music Between Us"?)

14 JIMMY

FOX News Special Edition – Flushing Meadows caught up with Bud Collins in his garden estate somewhere along the Connecticut coastline. Bud Collins was eager to get back to sports journalism and FOX News thought it more than right to bring him back from retirement. He agreed to interview for us Jimmy Connors, tennis legend and currently coach of tennis sensation Andy Roddick. Bud was able to interview Jimmy after an important match for Andy leading up to the men's finals.

Bud Collins: Marvelous James Scott Connors, tennis legend, sitting across from me, eye to eye, may I say hello.

Jimmy Connors: Hello, Bud. Welcome back.

Bud: Thank you. That was going to be my next line. Spectators across the country and those on cable television have not entirely lost track of you. You're active in the Master's Series (Editors' Note: The Master's Series is tennis's equivalent of life after professional retirement. A circuit exists for all age groups leading up to 75 years of age. Both men and women compete across the country. Life goes on for these professional players as if nothing ever happened, only they're a little bit slower.) But nobody thought you'd be back on centre court, in the bleachers, overlooking the progress of young protégé, Andy Roddick.

Jimmy: Well. It's a lucky coincidence that brought us together. We both live on the East Coast and we simply ran into each other while I was shopping for a dog leash. I was standing in an aisle looking for this leash and Andy was buying some dog food. We started talking.

This is about 6 months ago...

Bud: And the rest is history?

Jimmy: Well, we're not there yet. He's got a tough match ahead of him at this Open, but he's still progressing. It's not like I have to show him how to play tennis. He knows how to play. He knows how to play the game. It's now a question for him to make those decisions in his sport career that will allow him to be a champion. That's where I have my place as his coach.

Bud: That sounds all very interesting. Allow me to say this on television, but you were not always known for your rational attitude.

Jimmy: No. (EN: Laughing boyishly!) I had an attitude, but that was about it. I enjoy reading French literature, but I've always had trouble translating it into real life.

Bud: Hey, you've given Americans, no, you've given the world your talent, your eagerness to play; we don't expect you to be Marcel Proust. Let's leave that up to somebody else.

Jimmy: I mean I'm getting to that age (EN: Jimmy's kind of touchy about his age. There are discrepancies about his age, which is placed somewhere between 51 and 54) where I want to pass on something. It's something very personal. It's about transition (EN: Jimmy meant transmission). I mean I enjoy being in the limelight. Don't get me wrong. It's just that at my age it's not my tennis that's doing the talking any more.

Bud: What do you mean it's about transition?

Jimmy: Well, it's a complicated concept, especially in America. It's very different in Europe. I had a chance to discuss this with Andy's former coach, a Frenchman. Louis Malle. He wasn't a great tennis player in his time, except for a couple of Davis Cup finals. Of course, no offence meant. But, boy, was he able to pass on to Andy what tennis is all about. It's about angles, surface, ball velocity. It's mind-boggling what he taught Andy. And Andy took it all up like a sponge. He's got this awfully great potential with a theoretical marinade...We talked about it with Andy. Why doesn't all this lead to success? What I told him is that the circuit is his biggest enemy...

Bud: Have you ever been doped? Since John McEnroe has made his testimonial of having taken steroids, what has plagued other sports has become an ever more pressing question in tennis. Have you taken illicit drugs, James Scott?

Jimmy: No, I never have. Late in my active tennis career, I took advantage of many a medical advance. After long grueling matches, I used to get IV infusions to rehydrate, to recover more quickly. I had many massages to get over what seemed ever longer matches. I even did commercials for Nuprin (EN: A non-steroidal anti-inflammatory drug available without a prescription). But I never took any anabolic steroids. My temper tantrums were real! I particularly remember a match at the Open against John. It was on an historic day where Lendl played Pat Cash, Navratilova – Chrisi for the women's final, and in the late evening I was matched up against John in the semis. John showed this incredible stamina, but beyond that he showed this indifference to my best efforts, my best shots. I couldn't believe it. I really thought I was over the hill then.

Bud: Thank you for that honest response. Unfortunately this means that you don't have much to write about and so there won't be a book coming out on doping from you. Let's get back to the Bad Boy attitude. When Arthur Ashe commented for NBC, while following your late tennis career, he once said that you spent too much time pumping your arm, that such behaviour cost you too much, that it hurt you in the end. He was going against the All-American go out and get 'em attitude that you were exuding.

(EN: Jimmy Connors's wife steps in. Patti, former Playboy mate, hasn't aged since we first saw her in 1978 rooting for Jimmy, ever so reservedly.)

Jimmy: It may be hard to believe, but I've been a team player for a long time. Patti was a big support. Without her I would not have gone as far as I did. Most of my important lessons in life I learned in high school. My mother had taught me the game when I was very young. We started playing when I was 4 years old. I remember her very well, dressed in long flowing garments, like a white mirage. She even wore a light hat that protected her ears and neck. People thought that the tennis I learned wasn't serious because I had learned it from a woman. Of course, I proved them wrong. What really made a difference later on is what I learned during a junior high school (EN: Equivalent of middle school) during physical education. It was a gym week during which we played soccer. It wasn't yet popular for the girls, and half the boys hadn't even heard of it. Don't ask me why I was pretty good at it. Perhaps because of my English ancestry. My gene pool.

(EN: Bud's dozing off. It's understandable for an 80 year old geezer.)

Jimmy: Anyway, I was named captain of one of the teams. The rest of the class was divided into first picks, second picks, etc. At each pick, I had first choice and ended up, at each time, choosing the best of the crop. Chris Cooney and Mark Boonfield were my first and second picks. Those boys were golden. For goalie, I picked some tall guy, Danny Cannelloni. He had the startings of a beard and wasn't even 14 years old. Don't think he was doped though. Then there was my friend to be Jason. Another friend at the time I didn't pick and he looked at me really disappointedly when we finally started to huddle together as teams. Make a long story short. We sucked. I think we lost against all the other teams. There were three or four other ones if I remember well. Individually each player was the best in his category, but together we just weren't coordinating.

Bud: Sounds like you would have liked to disappear from the face of the earth.

Jimmy: Yes, a little. I was ashamed and would have given anything to be shrouded in a cloak of invisibility. In a sense, what I learned back then made me stronger, made me become a showman, but in a good sense. It's something I want to get through to Andy.

At this stage FOX News interrupts with a commercial.

15 IF I HAD DONE IT, THIS IS HOW IT WOULD HAVE HAPPENED

It must have been during a visit to Germany during the 1998 World Cup. I was spending a couple of days in Worms with friends of the family, seeing Martin Luther's house for the first time in the Medieval market square that was still very well conserved. Friends of family means that you know these people by virtue of your parents and that you probably would not have chosen them as your own friends. This being said, there was a strong connection to the Rumpelstilzens, the family I stayed with, as their son, an only son like myself, was about my age. I made this tremendous discovery while talking to them one evening. I don't know how we started speaking about my father. It's all a little hazy now and if it weren't for fiction, I'd never have picked up the pencil to write this. It must have been a conversation about divorce. The Rumpelstilzens almost had gone through their own divorce, but somehow had avoided it. Was it because they were Catholic, which was quite rare in this Protestant bastion of Germany? Catholics were known, to Protestants, as being able to tolerate certain infidelities better, leading to a higher success rate when it came to long lasting marriages; in any case, they told me, not about their infidelities, nor about the ways they had succeeded to stay together, but about their friends and how one couple after the other, over the years, had disintegrated. Frau Rumpelstilzen, whom I started calling by her first name by that time, complained about her friends who didn't know how to speak about anything else other than their awful husbands and how finally they had become liberated.

My parents had divorced at about the time the Rumpelstilzens were going through rough waters. Funny how my family was not able to stick together whereas the Rumelstilzens did. They had known my father quite well. Herr Rumpelstilzen had worked with him for many years selling automobiles. Before my father's death, they must have known each other for almost twenty years, though during this time they worked together only off and on so one would think that if he or his wife had any observations to share, these would have to be right on the money. My father died of cardiac arrest. A bypass surgery that had been performed a few days earlier had either gone awry or it wasn't effective enough in restoring proper cardiac function. It wouldn't be too difficult to identify the cause of death more precisely if I had access to autopsy reports, though I seriously doubt any was performed. My own understanding of his death is rather simplistic, and yet I always thought it to be the only explanation possible as it was the most likely, the most logical one. He died of a weak heart because he had spent his life drinking and smoking. At least a pack a day. Of cigarettes that is. In terms of beer, he drank more than a pack a day, and that don't include the heavy liquor. Never saw my Dad drunk. I heard him drunk once or twice. And remember seeing him very tranquilized by liquor, linked to a higher than usual alcohol intake and hence dose. What did him in, I thought, was that he drank every day and that he smoked every day. The Rumpelstilzens said to me that they had never known anybody who so deliberately did himself in. In other words, over the years, it seemed to be obvious to them, he committed a long suicide, and as all suicidal deaths he did it willingly and knowingly. That, of course, was news to me. Parents who have a death wish, I now would like to think, are like an algebraic formula that their kids cannot really solve. Parents put you into this world; how can they want to take themselves out of it? The cigarettes did it, the alcohol did it. My father, my mother used to say so insistently several years before the divorce, was sensitive. With what the Rumpelstilzens told me, I figured that he couldn't commit suicide in a violent way, but had long ago decided to leave this earth on his own account.

The bourgeois lifestyle has been criticised ever since it became more widespread in the 19th century. I'm not Marxist, nor do I belong to high society, but I was brought up in this milieu and somehow wonder if for all its comforts it hasn't also killed something in me. I remember one incident quite well when my father was home sick. This was quite rare. There was of course his double heart attack which he suffered in 1976, but from which he had not really recovered, but which did not seem to lead to scaling back on his work. There were also the kidney stones which had caused him tremendous pain. But the incident I'm talking about was unusual because he stayed at home without any apparent reason. He was under deep depression, I would say today, brought about by a mix of prescription drugs and alcohol. The smoking he was trying to quit, but he was a junky. My mother had hidden the cigarettes (what a stupid thing to do, and yet I think if she had thrown them away, she might have risked her life, and she knew it).

I came home in the afternoon and saw my parents struggling. Many years ago I still remembered what I had been doing that afternoon, playing soccer, spending play time with a friend? I walked into my parents' bedroom. My dad hadn't made an effort to dress for days and he was in his undershorts and undershirt, the kind you see in movies on European immigrants to the US who work long hours, have greasy skin and hairy chests, and who are known to beat their wives. In his white undergarments he seemed to blend into the bedroom surroundings. My parents' bedroom had large mirrors, white furniture, a white bed with white linens, white curtains, and that afternoon a bright light shone into the room, robbing the room of almost all contrast, leaving only my father's skin and my mother's dark voluminous hair. I can't remember anymore what exactly took place, I'm ashamed to say. Did he strike her? Did he grip her wrist? When I barged in on the scene, everything froze. I did. They did, though the look in my dad's eyes had been far away for days.

When he chased me through and out of the house in the following seconds, he did it like a zombie, not really looking. I was afraid. Not so much for myself, but for my mother and it is that that drove me by some force of nature back into the house.

Oh, I remember where we had been. We went to the orthodontist, my mother and I. And I slowly am realising that I'm switching things around. When we came home, my father started asking my mother about the cigarettes. He went to get them and she wanted to prevent him from it. He drove me out of the house. I was so proud to get back in. It was a day I had gotten my braces, a kind of rite of passage.

And I was able to scale the fence, from which I had fallen a couple of years earlier, almost breaking my neck. I ran down to the street and walked up the other side of the house into the apartment of my grandmother.

My grandmother wasn't a kind lady, though I loved her very much. She had been handicapped for a large part of her retired life, having strong diabetes and walking on crutches after a fracture in her leg went unnoticed. I hurried through her apartment and opened the door to my room. This door had not existed for very long. It had been built, so I was told and on this point I don't think there was much more to it, in order to combine my house with my grandmother's apartment for tax purposes. The door was open. Lucky me. I was so proud to make it back into the house as my father had chased me out at one end locking the garden door behind me. I've dreamt about this door many times. Perhaps it would have been better if it had been locked.

I hadn't said anything to my grandmother because, because I was more grown-up than before, because what could she do to help me being handicapped, because, and perhaps that's the real reason, I had to act fast. My mother was being held hostage by a zombie.

When I stepped back into the room, the scene I've already described took place, the fist around my mother's wrist, the frozenness, the dampened crying inwards of my mother. Oh my, what a mess.

My father was surprised to see me again. I don't think he expected to see me again and when he saw me the surprise was enough to make him stop.

I was lucky because being frozen, being as young as I was, I would have been no match even though he was under the influence. Today I would have called the police. I should have called the police. Domestic violence. I should have asked my grandmother to call as I don't think I knew how to. Didn't have that skill, call the police when you needed them. Wasn't that socially evolved. Keep things quiet, bourgeois to the core without knowing it. If only the door had been closed, it would have been necessary to call the police. Who knows, they might have been too late.

What if? Is a wonderful series of comic books in which the legends of Spiderman, the Fantastic Four, the Hulk and the likes are turned upside? For example, the Thing from the Fantastic Four never turns into the Thing and hence doesn't suffer from being an ugly monster for the rest of his life, without a gal. Or Spiderman, instead of being bitten by a spider, does nothing but pursue his physics degree, leaving it to someone else to be a superhero. What if I had murdered my father? Patricide.

I mean not premeditated murder, but meditated over years. Knowing what I knew about him committing a slow suicide, being in the situation I was where he threatened my mother, might I have taken him out right there and then, put him and us out of the misery? I probably could have covered the murder up, or even if charged, would have escaped prison, being a young minor. He wouldn't have married again. I wouldn't have a step sister...

16 THE INVISIBLE BAND

Illustration: The Invisible Man? Duran Duran's Simon LeBon performs in the music video for 1982's hit single "Rio ".

BAND'S DISAPPEARANCE SPARKS WONDER, OUTRAGE

By Scott Baker
Wed Sep 13, 4:39 PM ET

KANSAS CITY – If you blinked, you missed it. Members of the rock band "Duran Duran" are reportedly missing after a performance Tuesday night at Memorial Hall in Kansas City.

   Eyewitnesses attending the concert tell police that members of the legendary pop rock group donned what appeared to be mirrored coats and then simply vanished into thin air.

Jennifer Sanders, who was at the concert and witnessed the disappearance, tells reporters:

"Simon [the lead singer] was just singing the first part of 'Reach Up for the Sunrise"'.. you know 'so the time has come, the music's between us'.. and then they like just stopped playing and put on these shiny reflective coats. At first I was like 'okay, this is pretty cool' and then I asked my friend if she had any Tramadol in her purse because I forgot to bring mine, but then when I looked up again they were gone and I was all like 'what the eff?' So then I went into the bathroom because I had been holding it for so long and I just had this really weird feeling, you know like that feeling you get when you think someone's watching you?"

Some who were in attendance at the concert were angrier than others.

"I had been waiting since 'Big Thing' for a chance to see these guys in town," says Jason Donovan. "They finally get here and I'm having a great time, you know just loving it because it's true what they say, they're so much better live in concert, and then BAM!, they're gone. And I'm all like, 'what the eff?'"

Police have interviewed dozens of eyewitnesses for clues, but have been unwilling to release any information publicly. Some say there is intense speculation about the meaning of an unscheduled appearance that lead singer Simon LeBon made at the opening night of the musical "Rio", a Broadway adaptation of the group's runaway best selling album of 1982 by the same name. Cameras recorded an apparently intoxicated LeBon making a somewhat rambling statement to the audience:

"You know, it's been talked about before by a very wise man named Marcel Proust, I believe, about how we isolate ourselves... you know, from our own selves through all these various distractions and what not, such as the media and modern technology and just things like that. You know, we talked about that sort of thing on the wedding album about 'too much information' and so forth. Well, Rio is about something different than that: it's about a return to ourselves... a return to innocence, a return to nature. It captures the essence of savagery and of love, which of course I don't have to tell you people about because you already know how they're two opposite ends of the same spectrum. And so looking back, there wasn't a better time than that to capture what it was *really all about*. Maggie had just sent the British fleet to take over some islands which we Brits owned and Jimmy Connors had just managed to win the US Open, what a wonderful little savage he was. And of course we were getting ready to hit our prime time that year.. our sort of 'tiger tiger' moment... you know, this sort of cause and effect or 'yin and yang' if you will... you know, 'selling the Renoir and the TV set' and not wanting to be around when things got out, and that sort of thing. And so in the end when we made that album and we were putting the finishing touches on it and ramping up for the video shoot and everything, some friends of mine told me they were in production for the movie *The Philadelphia Experiment*, which showed how the US Navy managed to somehow warp time and space and make an entire friggin' *battleship* disappear into thin air just like that!"

Illustration: The USS Eldridge (DE-173) ca., subject of the 1984 film *"The Philadelphia Experiment"*.

"And I thought—and I told this to Nick as well and he agreed with me—you might as well make our video for Rio into this sort of 'counterweight' to all of that savagery as it were, and you can well imagine it's so very gratifying to see that our work is finally getting all the recognition that it has truly deserved all these wonderful years. And hasn't it been a long time coming, ladies and gentlemen? I mean, it's like we disappeared along with that battleship back then for all you ever knew or cared about. Well anyway, let me end on this memorable note... yes she truly does still dance on the sand, and on behalf of the academy I'd like to encourage everyone to keep 'reaching up for the sunrise'. And now on with our little show."

Editor's note: the Eldridge was a destroyer escort, not a battleship as Mr. LeBon has claimed.

Police authorities intend to continue their investigation about the mysterious disappearance of Duran Duran in front of a live audience, and have asked anyone with any kind of information about their whereabouts to get into contact with them immediately.

"We're treating it as a missing persons case," says Detective Steve Hahn of the Missing Persons Unit in Kansas City. "We're asking for anyone with any kind of information about what might have happened that night to please step forward and let us know. You can even reach us anonymously if you would prefer. Please folks, help us find Duran Duran. They were due out for another album soon and I own all of their albums up to this point."

17 HERCULES AND THE CLOAK OF INVISIBILITY

Part II

"No, Frank, I'm afraid that ONCE AGAIN you got it wrong." Hercules said, shaking his head in disbelief. "How can one person be so wrong so many times? I don't know, it bewilders me."

"It what?" Frank looked at Hercules, eyes squinting.

"It bewilders me Frank."

Frank still looked confused.

"It CONFUSES me Frank. It CONFUSES me as to how one person could rack up such a record of being so wrong so many times. It's almost superhuman. It's almost as if I'm standing here looking at someone who is not a human, Frank. Congratulations."

Frankie cracked a smile and puffed his chest out a little. "Well, thank you very much Hercules. I don't believe you've ever said anything as nice as that to me ever before."

Hercules turned away so that the superhuman wouldn't see the look of resignation on his face. Frankie never seemed to disappoint did he, Hercules thought. After a moment of silence and Frank basking in the glow of what he perceived to be a compliment, Hercules collected his thoughts again.

"Anyway, it's no big deal Frank. So the cloak of invisibility is not stain-proof, but I can always clean it up and no one will ever know you spilled anything on it."

Frankie thought about it for a moment. "I still maintain that you told me that it was stain-proof. I swear I heard it."

Hercules raised his arms in the air, as if surrendering. "You're right

Frank, you're right. I did say that. I told you it was stain-proof. You're right, it's stain-proof. Because that was one of the most important criteria I had in mind when I was designing the thing. It was either going to be that or bullet-proof, and I just figured 'what the Hell, why not protect against coffee and wine stains first?' So just go ahead and spill whatever you want on it Frank. It really doesn't matter to me."

Frankie smiled. He knew Hercules had told him that. "I knew it!" he exclaimed.

"Anyway, where is the cloak, Frank? Do you have it with you," Hercules asked, as he picked up one of his inventions: a gyroscopic coffee cup holder. Frank had asked for one because he was always spilling coffee in his car, reasoning that at least with a gyroscopic holder, he could go so far as to roll his vehicle over in a horrendous crash and yet there would be his coffee, still in its holder, waiting to be sipped. The invention seemed very à propos to the conversation at hand and so Hercules fumbled with it for a bit. He noticed that Frank still hadn't answered his question though.

"Frank, the cloak.. where is it?"

Frank's eyes shifted to the left and to the right. His lips were pursed together. He looked like a kid who was trying to hide something.

"The cloak, Frank!"

"The cloak?" Frank finally said. "It's... well... I was going to tell you about that."

This didn't sound good already, Hercules thought. "Yes?.." he asked.

"Well... you see... I had to... to loan it to somebody."

"You did what Frank? You LOANED it to somebody?" Hercules asked in disbelief. "But Frank I explicitly told you NOT to loan it to anybody!"

"I know, I know you said that. I remember. You're right, you did tell me that, but listen..."

Hercules raised his hands and said "this better be good".

"It is good, you're going to like it. It's good, trust me. You know that band Duran Duran?"

Hercules' eyes were fluttering, wondering what the Hell Duran Duran could possibly have to do with any of this.

"Yes, I've heard of them. Why?"

"Well you see. I'm friends with some friends of theirs – guy named Armani but no difference, friends of theirs – and I was telling them about this special cloak- I mean coat- I had."

"You're telling other people about this??" Hercules asked incredulously.

"No Herc, I didn't tell them about what it does or nothing. I just told them they were expensive high-fashion coats and that I wanted them to try them on. I figured at least Nick Taylor would want to try one on. Did I ever tell you they're my favorite group? So because they're my favorite group and I thought... well I thought maybe I would get a chance to meet them and everything."

Hercules didn't like where this was going. "And so?..."

"Well... and so I says to this guy 'hey, have them try these things on and get back to me.'"

"And get back to you huh."

"That's right, try 'em on and get back to me, let me know how they look and feel."

"Like that matters Frank? And so they did, or what happened?"

"Here," he pulled out a magazine, "you can read about it for yourself."

Frank handed the magazine to Hercules, opened up to the story about Duran Duran.

"'Duran Duran explains mysterious disappearance'," Hercules began reading. His reading became barely audible as he browsed the article. His lips moved and he whispered as he read "'so we tried it out, we put them on and then we were like, *teleported* into another world you know. It was like Star Trek or something'.. oh Jesus, Star Trek!"

"You like Star Trek?" Frankie asked. Hercules ignored him and kept reading.

"I like Star Trek," Frank answered his own question.

"OH JESUS!" Hercules suddenly cried out as he read the article... "'and so I gave mine away to Jimmy Connors'..? Jimmy Connors?? Simon LeBon gave the cloak away to Jimmy Fucking Connors Frank??! That's great.. Wonderful news. Now we're screwed. Good job Frank."

Frank had a sour look on his face as if he might cry.

"Jimmy Connors, Frank," Hercules repeated.

He let the words soak in for a while. Frankie's eyes began to swell and a tear formed in the corner of his left eye.

"I'm sorry," he whimpered.

Hercules regained his composure and felt a little bad for yelling at him. After all, the big guy was crying now. But then, that wasn't too unusual.

"Look, it's okay Frank. We'll just try to get it back then, okay?"

Frank nodded his head up and down, not looking at Hercules, still saddened because he did a bad thing.

"And the other cloaks Frank? Do the other band members still have theirs? Because we need them all back now."

"I think so," was all Frank could say.

Hercules paused for a moment to think. Was it the end of the world if one or more cloaks were lost? Probably not. But it *was* his greatest invention, and the tireless work of so many years.

"Look Frank, let me explain something to you," Hercules began. "The cloak that I gave to you to try out can be used for good *or* evil. We just have to be careful who gets their hands on it, understand?"

Frank seemed to cheer up a bit. "But... but *we're* evil, aren't we Herc?"

"You're not that evil, Frank, don't kid yourself," Hercules answered, seeing the gleam of a drying tear in Frankie's eye. "But there's more to it than that, Frankie. It's not all just about good and evil. It's about the fulfillment of a man's hopes and aspirations. You see, all my life Frank, I've been trying to create the cloak of invisibility. Growing up, I had no mother and a father who disowned me. I wanted to be invisible. I wanted to disappear from this planet. There was too much injustice on the planet Frank. So I determined that I either had to beat it... or join it. In school I determined that no matter what happened, my life would not be complete until I created it. So I studied HARD, Frank. I mean I learned all I could. I was an honors student, straight A's, all that. But you see, my parents never had the 'my kid is smarter than your kid' bumper sticker Frank. Oh no, it wasn't that easy for me. Sit right down in that chair and let me tell you a story about some of what I had to go through. You see buddy, you're not the only one with stains on your record..."

18 THE GRIMELS

Where they came from exactly was a hotly contested topic at the local Starbucks. After years of noble late-night discourse, the origins were defined as follows: The industrial god, Usiphues, created them after one storm-laden night. In the wake of dawn, the Grimels had somehow managed to grow out of the cotton ridges of his slippers through the mere action of Usiphues's buggers which had a habit of dropping in and around his bed, including into his slippers which were neatly arranged close to his bed, pointing in the direction of the toilet. Though no one had ever seen them, the mere fact that their origins were established seemed to give a fair amount of credence to their existence. That a description of them also existed, with multiple fine details as you will now see, is even more striking. Imagine them. They were not much taller than the slippers and looked like they were shrouded in a fencing outfit, but with robes on the lower half of their bodies so that you couldn't see their feet. Like a fencer's mask would look, they had no eyes. Old World lore had it that because they had no eyes, they had the power to be invisible. Being blind, what otherwise would have been a handicap, turned out to be in their favour. It is difficult to say if we have any proof of these powers. Since no one has ever seen a Grimel, one could conclude that it is because of these powers to be invisible, but this would be a bit too easy.

However, another element in their story would be proof at least that they were blind. Also, by knowing that they carried sabres the fencing bit would be supported. They seemed also not to have any ears, and no visible mouth; they were rumoured to communicate through a kind of hieroglyphic code that was written in the form of tables. These tables were etched into stone or paper or whatever was available. A Grimel who wanted to talk to another Grimel would use his sabre to point to the code and the other Grimel would somehow perceive what was said. Since Grimels were blind, they could not see what part of the code was pointed to, so they were not able to understand what was said visually. The code and the way of communicating this way were virtual, a kind of primitive computer.

Much was not known about Grimels and every time someone wanted to know more or ask questions, it was said that the Grimels were waiting for a kid to interpret their raison d'etre. They were waiting for a kid to not only explain their existence to others, but enlighten them on their existence, make them understand who and why they are. It was said that because many fencing terms to this day remained in French that this child would know how to speak French. It was further rumoured that the child would be versed in the arts of the Cloak and Dagger movies so popular in the Old World, giving work to many starving fencing artists and athletes.

One single footnote: Grimels are said to have sewn the cloak of invisibility with their small sabres. Their workmanship is considered to be of the highest calibre. It appears that the cloak's characteristics come from two things: the material that was used and the Grimels' stitch pattern, which must stem from or be otherwise linked to their language.

Who's wearing the pants?

1.
Upon returning home, I put my new pants on my head
Wasn't sure of the size, wanted to try them as quickly as possible
There was no other way to try them than to wear them like a hat
When you're fat and the midsection is thick
You may say why not change your pants then
Get a bigger pair; well, I love this pair; the color's just right.

2.
Then I ask the advice of my cat because it's spring
And the color's just right and the cat says
"What do you worry about, live your life like the birds,
I reckon they barely remember last spring's call
And if they do, they better watch out or I'll bite their head off."
Split-up, lonely adult influence, I say the cat's right.

3.
"How come you are having a conversation with our cat about
   birds, Dad?"
"Because I'm a veterinarian."
"And why do you wear those new pants on your head?"
"I don't have to wear them on my head all the time.
I can slip them back in the box they came, but,
Son, now that the cat is out of the sack,
Let me tell you, it's not only my profession, but my passion
To talk with our cat and wear pants on my head."

19 PIEROGI TIME

It was the usual crowd in there on a Monday morning, the women stocking up for the week on their kielbasa and the fixings for their babkas and their pierogis. A lot of Polish people all in there speaking their Polish language, but I wasn't one of them. I didn't speak Polish, and I only lived in this Polish community because the rent was cheaper. Coming to the New World, I found I could influence the amount that went out of my pocket just by picking the area where a certain ethnic group lived, unlike back home, where no matter where you lived, it was all pretty much the same, with little variation in costs. Oh sure, you could choose a poorer neighborhood, but there was no place like this melting pot called America, where everyone lived together: black, white, Jew, Pole, Germanic, and Hispanic, all blended together like a thick and spicy potato soup.

I went to the counter with my goods, two bags in all. I stood in line behind a lady who was chatting it up with the proprietor. It was obvious they knew each other. I could tell by the friendly sounds of that foreign banter, and the universal language of laughter, that they knew each other quite well. I'd seen her in here a few times before. She was a regular. Then a thought occurred to me. If I'd been in here enough times to know she was a regular, wasn't I also a regular? I laughed quietly at the idea of becoming a regular at a small Polish grocery store here in the New World. What would the people back home think of me? Perhaps they would laugh too. They'd probably advise me to learn some Polish as well. Not a bad idea, I thought, as the two finished up their conversation and said their widzenias.

The friendly gentleman behind the counter said hello to me in English and rang up my items. Two cans of spinach, a pound of ground beef, a half-gallon of milk, a loaf of French bread. I was in luck because the extra sharp cheddar cheese was on sale, so I purchased a block of that as well. I finished up with three liters of water, knowing it was supposed to get hotter later in the day and I didn't want to be caught having to drink the corroded pipe-laden tap water. The water in my apartment building always had an odor, and I was advised by a tenant who knew about such things that the owners had failed their city health code inspection and were required to make some repairs, but had not yet done so. The gentleman behind the counter methodically packed my groceries before ringing me up.

"Five-five-one, please," he said, announcing the bill. Five dollars and fifty-one cents was the total bill. I loved how my dollars went farther in this friendly little community. I would have paid them twice that much just for the courtesy they always seemed to display. They were a happy lot. Even in their poverty they were a happy lot. I dug around in my pockets, looking for a penny. The gentleman smiled as I paid him with exact change.

"Thank you," he said in English.

"Thank you, do widzenia," I answered back.

"Do widzenia," he smiled.

As I left the tiny grocery store there were others coming in: more ladies stocking up on provisions for their families. It was ritualistic, and it gave me a satisfied feeling that things were going as they should go; that all was right with the world, and that happiness prevailed. I thought about how similar it was to the Old World. Even though the language they spoke was different, it was still the same, and I realized that this desire for routine and the comfort of life in the Old World had drawn me to this community even more so than what I used to believe was my reason: simple economics. In fact I was willing to pay more to live here, only I didn't have to. Not having to pay more was just an added benefit to the community appeal. The real reason I was drawn to this little town was the friendly people and the old-fashioned lifestyle.

No sooner had I concluded that the town's lifestyle was the draw than another thought occurred to me, only this one seemed less pure and innocent: perhaps I was drawn to live here *because* I couldn't understand these people. Maybe, I thought, by not being able to understand them, I could imagine that it was all just neighborly banter and harmonious living. The reality might have actually been that they were smiling so widely at me because they thought of me as a guest in their home. Whatever the reason, it didn't matter, and I was content to go on living here for a while. It provided some comfort.

I needed comfort. Ever since my wife had died, it was hard to go on like normal. I had to get out and get away. I had to move somewhere: it really didn't matter where, so long as nobody knew me, and I didn't know anybody. Certainly these nice Polish people were not going to inquire about me or the reasons for my being here. They didn't care so much about my occupation as they did that I was a nice, quiet man who paid his bills on time and never made a fuss about anything. I had to lay low for a time: I had to hide out until it was safe to be seen again. So I packed my bags and said goodbye to the Old World. I made a new start, doing private investigative work. After all, there are good guys and bad guys everywhere you go. The world never runs out of them, and the money can be just as good here as anywhere else. Living in that picturesque Polish community had been ideal cover. I suppose it was just another reason for living there, though the fact that everyone was so friendly seemed like an even better reason for living there.

Then I got the call from an old friend. He said he needed to speak with me, and that it was a matter of some urgency. I put away my groceries and sped off to go meet him. The tires on my Maserati squealed as burning rubber made clouds of black smoke, and sand kicked up in the faces of the women shopping for provisions.

20 DEAR JACK, A LETTER FROM THE BAHAMAS

The Bahamas, 17 May 2007

Dear Jack, excuse me for, I was once told never to start out with an excuse-me, whatever the occasion, giving a speech, making a comment or writing an email, but here it goes for lack of a more thoughtful way of starting out a letter, excuse me for writing to you as Jack, your first name. It's my professional conscience that's getting in the way. It so often does. Though we have run into each other quite a lot lately, was it at Osco's where we both have worked or in the supermarkets around town. I don't remember you proposing that we refer to each other by our first names, and yet when writing letters how much easier, how much more immediately does it become possible to do so? As if all the rules changed, conventions that keep people at a distance overturning with every word that is written.

Thanks for your letter dated 3 March 2007 in which you mention Richard's death. How many times have I thought about his passing away without being able to imagine any other terms to describe his death. How cold, how final this word is I only begin to realize.

Perhaps, as you say, have I been only too content to concentrate on my work, ignore what was happening around me. There's nothing more addictive than one's work and ambitions. Richard and I were close; we spent many an evening together, discussing our young plans for life, the ones we had been discussing since our high school days. I agree with you that in many respects he was insensitive, not so much in dealing with others, but in that he suppressed his own feelings. Have you heard of the rapper Eminem, of course, who hasn't? His childhood was marked by a drunken mother, an absent father, and a neighborhood as violent as no other? His early compositions express all his pent up emotions; his are cries of anguish, of disappointment and bitterness, stale in the night. How many evenings did I spend like that dreaming into the night, sometimes in company of another, many times on my own, forlorn but free.

Tonight I came home late after closing the pharmacy. I ate a salad though I've heard it's not good to eat raw vegetables late at night. I was in no mood to go to bed and sat in front of the television, debating if I should turn it on. Glad that I did, I stumbled upon an old Jerry Lewis film. I don't know the title, but it's the one where he works in a department store, getting into all kinds of trouble. I missed the beginning and joined in only seconds before that famous scene where he's playing air-typewriter. The scene is set to music, and though the film itself is no masterpiece (I would argue that some of his films could be considered as such), this scene is an absolute joy. He wears that red sweater and with his hair slicked back he looks so much like the stereotypical good boy of the 1950's, full lips and all. This week I've been catching up on...homework, I was almost going to say. It's true, I've been studying on the side, doing some continuing education as a correspondence course. How did I let myself get suckered into doing it this way? It's a shame. I should have been more vigilant. These correspondence courses are listed with the Better Business Bureau in almost all of the major American cities because of the false advertisement, the false promises, with which they lure innocent people eager to get ahead in life or to further educate themselves into their web of high-priced courses full of garbage. Anyway, I've been busy with this, but finally got around to writing to my aunts and uncles in the Other World. One of them had a birthday and another one was pregnant and close to giving birth. As we speak, she might have labor pains. I thought it would be a nice gesture to write her a letter to tell her I was thinking of her. By the way, when I received your letter, Jack, I realized that your letter meant you were thinking of me and however lonely my life was because someone was thinking of me, it was worth living. However long, however short that will be.

I end here, Jack, and wish you relaxing holidays. Take a break from the mountain biking. It ain't kosher 5 pennies worth, and might render your retinas more fragile!

Yours truly, Rita "Babe"

21 MOVING ON

I
The Philadelphia Papers – 20 years on

The bus stop was really much more than that: there were twenty or so bus lines whose regular routes took its users into all directions. Not bad really for a city of 20,000. The city seemed that much larger, that much more accessible. It was a rare occurrence to have Anna alone. Had she missed her bus? Had she intended to take a later one because she had to run some errands in the city? Normally, like perhaps most 12 year olds, she was surrounded by her two best friends, Kasha and Irene, neither of which could one easily take a liking to. One had a boy's face and the other a whiny voice. How could anyone be faulted for not liking them? First of all, they were always around, as if protecting Anna from any unwanted advances. Most of all, Kasha had told on Brian.

Saturday morning school just ended: they had just left class, a couple of hours of sports. The bus wouldn't leave until well after one o'clock so they had a couple of hours to kill. The girls were full of ideas, wanting to go to the ice cream parlor. This was the case more often than not. The older boys were also becoming adept at finding something commercial to do in the city such as buy records of the latest English pop music import. Duran Duran albums were bought because the older brother had heard of them; Phil Collins was doing a cover of a Supremes classic, "You Can't Hurry Love." They sang along to these titles as much as their two years' worth of foreign language skills, limited to the class room and little application outside of it, allowed them to do. It was the sheer hunger for anything new and even slightly exotic.

By that time Brian knew he would be leaving, forever. He would leave the city where he was born, move out and into the wide world, and never return the same again. Could it have been that which pushed him to betray the confidence of Anna which she had placed in him, many moons earlier, when she had told him about Gerhard and how she was thinking about going steady?

"Why doesn't she speak to me? Why will I remember only that picture of her, sitting down, quiet, refusing eye contact?"

Brian knew why those many moons earlier she had told me all that. She wanted to see his reaction. She must have had a hunch by then that he liked her. Oh, that Gerhard! He was a grown boy almost, so unlike himself, skinny, dressed by Mom. Tennis shoes, he knew about, they were neatly placed in his dresser, but they were worn when you played tennis, not at school casually. Since there were very few extracurricular activities, difficult to imagine for an American reader, either he was at school, playing tennis, or at home, where he usually wore house shoes when he wasn't off playing soccer. There was no other time to be filled with anything, but waiting for the bus.

Anna was sitting on the floor where hundreds of people walked over and by every day. She was a tall girl, easily one head taller than he. Big-boned would not be a kind description; yet, her proportions were not the same as his. She had a lovely face, big glasses, bangs, blond hair, and kissable cheeks. On the day he had to say good-bye to her, she wore jeans with a matching vest of a deep blue. The jeans were cut for a woman, large at the hips and crept short at the ankles. Her short socks were showing when she was sitting down. She didn't look at him; it was a comfort to him many years later to think that she might have cried.

But let's not get carried away. They were mature enough to actually say good-bye. It would be the last memory he had of her, of being alone with her, and for a long time it was perhaps the most romantic thing that happened to him. She was angry because he had shared with others what she had told me in private. "Why had I done it? Out of confidence because I was leaving?"

Maybe he was jealous, of the other boys, the ones with more muscles. Maybe he was just proud of being able to show that he had remembered what she told me, that it had touched me deeply. In the end, I think it was the showing off in front of the others, that they knew that he was the one she had confided in and that he was leaving them behind, they who knew nothing about her because they didn't love her like he did. It was a competition which he was bound to lose because he was leaving; he would be ostracized by the group; he had to mark his last point. It's understandable that she would not speak to him anymore. It was a terrible rejection, worse than if she had made reproaches. On the scale of other human events and dramas, of murder, this betrayal seemed not so terrible.

"What was she going to say anyway? That she preferred bigger boys and that I never had a chance."

They had hovered around each other, sitting in different places, her sitting straight-legged, looking off into the distance, perhaps looking for some one whom she knew, whom she could wave to and call to come by, him standing, his mind hovering in a void. They had set the time aside to talk, but didn't find the words. He would remember some birds landing on the green areas outside the bus stop building, the bank that was inside the building and the area where she sat, not far from the bank entrance, just opposite from a candy and tobacco store. It was gray like the city birds. If tears had been shed, they would have dissolved the concrete underneath their feet and around them because the tears were acidic. If they dissolved concrete, they also dissolved any feelings she had ever had for him.

II
"Stars in the Spanish Morning" – Profession: Literary Critique

It doesn't pay much. It doesn't really pay anything at all, Jim was thinking to himself. Here he was, reading and re-reading high school poetry magazines, critiquing the writing, giving scores in a nationwide contest, whose end was in sight. He was one amongst many other high school English teachers who had entered themselves to participate in the literary critiquing. There were a couple of teachers in his department, but they never found the time to talk about this activity. Maybe they just didn't want to be bothered any further.

He had never been a big fan of creative writing classes. He gave one himself, but he might as well have been teaching Shop or Wood. The themes that would be worked on, here they were, became visible in the same manner. It didn't matter much if you were reading a glossy magazine from California or a minimalist black and white covered one from New York. The resemblance was surprisingly striking. The texts would take the shape of poetry and short stories mostly.

It was on a Saturday afternoon; his wife was doing the grocery shopping and he started to read a story named "Stars in the Spanish Morning." The titles were written in cursive; this text took up two-thirds of a page and was written in the first person, an account of a student visiting Spain for the summer. He liked the title. When he was young, he had been to the Balearic Islands and had kept pleasant memories from that time. It was a very short story about him (he assumed it was a man) meeting a girl named Laura.

He liked the way she was described. The barrette that pulled back her hair, the yellow-dyed T-shirt fitting close to her body. Though the theme of adolescent angst in relationships was quite present in all stories and though it could be a very rich theme, he was and would always be surprised at such candor, such precision in physical description, and the energy with which such an encounter was lived.

"Laura, what a pretty name! Was that her real name?," he was thinking to himself.

This had to be a real story. The encounter described almost did not take place. The two met in their dormitory, but could not leave the building. Instead, they went up on the roof. Resignation was not going to get the better of them. Then they started talking. They had, what the author said was, a conversation. And that's where Jim lost a little of his interest.

He would have liked to hear what they had to say to each other. He was an older man, who also was attached to the significance and power of particular words. The mere presence of words was not enough. He needed to hear a particular rhythm, have a particular order respected to be transported. While reading this story almost to the end, he lost the string in the story.

"Who cared about the stars that were the same to everyone, when he could not hear what they said to each other?"

He was enraged because he had been drawn into their story and then realized his folly because to get so worked up over a very short story was not going to get him anywhere. Neither was he going to finish his quota in two months' time, nor was he ever going to grow into a respected literary critic by approaching a text so blindly. Was this going to pay his bills? Instead of stepping back a moment, he relished in hatred for the story. For some brief moments, he had been in Spain with them. But where in Spain had they been? The author neglected to state this all important detail. The author had thought that to give the name of the girl was important whereas Jim, the critic, would have more than appreciated to know the name of the city.

He ended up scribbling down his critique in a small section on the grading sheet when his wife returned. "Can you help with the bags?" The story remained with him as if it was something he didn't quite digest. What was it, but a lovely story about a shared moment? The city couldn't be named Laura.

III
Led Zeppelin Reunites – London

Laura wore perfume that evening. David could have commented on her smelling good. It would have been a way to let her know that he leaned in when she talked, that he paid attention, that the familiar operated between them, but why bother? He could have asked her about the brand, but he always thought that it was rather ill-behaved to ask that of a woman. He considered such a question sacrilege and almost as unforgivable as asking a woman's age. He kept quiet. He had to pay attention closely and leaned in; getting a whiff of the perfume once or twice during the hour they spent together walking through the neighborhood.

When he decided that they would not leave the congress center to travel back into the city, in some vain attempt to make something of the evening, she listened, so they kept walking around in the congress center.

As all congress centers must be in the world, this one was quite deserted at night. An urban renewed wasteland, with disenchanted youth lingering about, and yet it should be given a name for the sake of completeness. Excel, or something of the like. It was located in the Docklands, at Royal Victoria docks, with the old ship cranes painted black, a reminder of the Thames' past, sculptural, imposing in the lighted night. Painted Black? Even in this sterile place, there were echoes of the glorious Stones. They went on a metal bridge to cross the river. It had been built only a few years earlier. It was a pedestrian bridge, suspended high in the sky. The curious thing was that once you were on the bridge you realized that you were only a few sky yards from the takeoff runway from London City Airport.

All that they saw around them. The scenery seemed to seep into their conversation and fill the gaps. She spoke to him about being shut up in an ATM teller once at university. The lights around them were impressive; the elevators that took them up to the middle part of the bridge startled him when the motors were set into motion. He let himself be carried, without getting carried away. He had no plan other than to be a perfect gentleman and not let his cold get any worse. He told her about how he liked the sodium lights, how they reminded him of Chicago, of his glory days, as they entered the residential part of the water front.

It was cool that evening, for London standards; only some kilometers away the Led Zeppelin reunion took place under what was formerly called the Millennium Dome (the O_2 dome). He would have liked to have seen them. Some journalists described it as an epic reunion. A few were courageous enough to say that they should hang it up. It didn't rain, that was a plus. Laura and David ended up going through parts of the neighborhood (tiny, proper individual houses) before going back to the other side. The second time on the bridge he saw a sign that before filming on location, rights had to be granted; the setting was quite cinematographic. He felt watched all of a sudden, and it made him self-conscious as if their conversation needed to be as epic as a Hollywood movie, where every little detail takes on weight. One journalist described the reunion as a success because Led Zep didn't fall into the same trap as other aging rockers; instead of speeding up their numbers, rushing through them to get to the end; they slowed down and the impact was one of weight, of measured power. Redemption? Who knows? Led Zeppelin's pretty cool, but it's not like the Goldberg Variations.

Once all the way on the other side, out on the parking lot in front of the center, they spoke about their parents, or was it her brother, or was it about something else. There was the large open area in front of the main congress hall, with blue Christmas lights in the small trees set next to their hotels a little off from the main entrance which seemed far off on the other side; there were some more restaurants, that somehow seemed deserted too or foreboding, making them think about the first restaurant which seemed preferable but which they had passed on as well (it had exotic looking waitresses in it, as it was a theme restaurant; the outfits were probably included in the price, how could they not be judging by those prices!).

They saw a day care center on the way back. The lighted windows gave an even greater impression of transparency as if in their day and age it was no longer possible to keep and educate kids without lots of light and lots of windows so that a worried parent could look in if he wished. They just kept walking and entered the front lobby. Then she said it was time to go to bed. He left then. The next morning they met for work.

IV
Refusal to accept – Another country

Laura hadn't quite understood what he had said over the phone. Brian had said something about loving another woman, in another country. She had perhaps tuned out by then. He may have said her name even. She felt cheated, not so much because he loved another woman, but because he announced this over the phone. She had thought his manners impeccable; it was one of the traits that had attracted her to him initially and still did. She had to go see him, not because she was angry with him, but she wanted to hear it from him directly. A kind of sado-masochistic thing, she knew it could come to no good.

It was a late fall evening on the South Side of Chicago. She would take the bus; she appreciated only to have put on a sweater. It was a favorite sweater of hers, not yet known to him. It's a beautifully woven, off-white American Indian-patterned sweater. Taking the bus allowed her to leave the jacket behind. The city lights sped by; she was only minutes from arriving at his apartment. The word "Rejection" started to take shape in her mind and take hold of her heart. Adept of women's magazines, she imagined the word as the title of a future piece on the subject. Maybe written by her? Imagining the helpful hints of how to cope with it, she began to adopt some kind of strategy.

She would make him regret it. She didn't even care anymore to hear it in person from him. She didn't want to talk. She wanted her wonderful sweater to harbor her, hand-knit, white in the dim light with a colorful central pattern, clinging to her skin.

She took the earphones off. Yes was playing. The Police, another group he had introduced her to. He had varied taste; she had been to a jazz piano concert with him, but had fallen asleep. Sting she knew, but she hadn't heard of his group from before. She had even told Brian that he looked a little like Sting. He was flattered. She didn't mean to flatter him, but she let it pass. She was in love again. Arriving at the apartment building, she checked in at the front desk. She felt watched. Maybe her sweater was attractive after all. He came down to sign her in and they went upstairs.

Many years later, she thought about him every so often. Would he remember her? She no longer had any feelings for him, and yet it was a comfort of sorts, a thought of thoughts, to believe that he did. Would he, living in a new country, remember the times they spent in restaurants, living like kings, remember her? Would he, years, many years later, finally understand that she loved him once? She was in her world, and he in his. They were like skewed lines not to meet again.

22 A LES TOURELLES

It was all over now, and Joan felt a strange mix of excitement and yet deep regret. Only hours before, she had led her newly confident men onto a charge to capture the two English fortresses surrounding Orleans. They had routed the English in a battle that few had expected and whose outcome even fewer could believe. She and her men could finally relax now and recover from the battle. They feasted on a victory meal of beef soaked in red wine, tasting all the more sweet for the moment at least, as they relished in their unimaginable victory. And yet it was regret she found that came seeping into her mind, as she considered everything that was lost. The last thing she had wanted to do was draw blood from the enemy, or to see her own men fall. But the English had refused to surrender, and so she did what she felt compelled to do.

"Twas a great victory, my maiden," Francois Chevalier said as he savored his meal. "Simply *incroyable*."

"Ouais, just wait until M. Duke of Bedford learns all about this!" another soldier enthusiastically added.

"Not so fast," was Joan's reply. "We should not be celebrating the deaths of those men. You should confess if you have done so. I myself will need to confess for the many terrible things I've done today." She began to sink in sadness. Seeing her depressed state of mind, her soldiers became confused.

"But dear Joan, you have done nothing but good today! You have given us a great victory! And now we can rest. It should be enough to scare the English, no? Peut-etre we should wait for them to leave now?"

Joan marinated on what the soldier said, and continued to chew on her steak. It struck her that the idea of waiting around for the English to leave simply wasn't going to do.

"No, Jean-Marie, we cannot just wait for them to leave. We must bring the fight to them! We must bring the fight to the English if we are to win back our country! Our gentle Dauphin will be coronated in Reims! I suggest you dismiss all talk of waiting around and hoping for things to change. The English will *never* leave, don't you understand? The Burgundians and the English will never give us back that which is rightfully ours!"

Hearing this, the soldiers knew that the break in the battle would be a short-lived one. The girl had inspired those around her with her optimism, her certainty, and her sense of urgency. If she were truly given to the French people as a gift from God, then they were in for a much longer struggle than any of them would have believed only the day before, for the struggle against the English would not be won so easily.

Joan continued. "And tomorrow we shall warn the defenders at Les Tourelles to please surrender to us, for we mean them no harm. However, should they refuse to surrender, we will be forced to evict them."

"Evict them? You mean by force of arms?" Jean-Marie asked, guardedly.

"Yes, Jean-Marie, by force of arms, whatever is necessary we shall do. Believe me, it's the last thing I want to do, but somehow we've got to get those redcoats to leave us to our land."

Francois Chevalier seemed taken aback. Her use of the term 'redcoat' was a strange way to describe an Englishman.

"My dear maid, excuse me but... uh, why did you call the Englishmen 'redcoats'? Some sort of secret code is it?"

Joan stopped in mid-chew. She realized she said something that she meant to keep to herself. She decided it was best to simply spill the beans and let the chips fall where they may. Not that the beans were chips, but you know what I mean.

"*Okay.....*" she began in dramatic fashion. "You're probably not going to believe *any* of this. I mean, I know I wouldn't if I were you. But it's true, every word of it, just as I swear on this Bible that I'm using as a hot pad right now. You see, one day when I was just a little girl, I was visited by this little faerie. No, not Richard Simmons. It was a magical little faerie, like the kind you read about in fairy tales. He was gaily skipping down the road as faeries are wont to do. I said hello to him and he stopped in his tracks. I think I scared the little guy because he immediately maced me with his pixie dust and I was temporarily blinded. Couldn't see a thing. But I began to feel something. I became light as a feather. It was as if I was being lifted out of this world. There was a lightness and a goodness which permeated my body, and all I could feel was love. I was transformed into pure energy. But I could still hear the little faerie's voice. He said to me 'Joan, you have a very important mission. We need you to conquer France for us and kick out the English. Take the King to Reims for his coronation. This is your sacred mission Joan. Don't fail us.' Well, naturally I was shocked. I was amazed! I had only heard a few things about the English from what my uncle had told me. Also, our village had been burned once before. But besides that, I was not very aware of what had been happening to our dear France. Then the voice told me to open my eyes. There before me were the Saints Michael, Catherine, and Margaret – all three of them! They were smiling at me. I had thought it was the faerie talking to me but it was not, it was them. They went on to say 'Joan, when the time comes, we will prepare for you a suit of armor which will protect you from all harm. Wear this armor, Joan. It was stitched together by the Grimels.' 'The Grimels?' I asked. 'Yes, the Grimels. Wear it and lead your men to glorious victory, in the name of France, Joan. Or else we'll all be eating fish and chips for breakfast.' Well, I was not about to say no to the saints, so I agreed to their terms, but not before making sure they knew what they were talking about. 'And how do I know you're telling me the truth?' I asked. They answered 'We're saints Joan, would we lie to you? We've helped out many people such as yourself, who find themselves as the chosen ones. The chosen ones must be chosen, they cannot be volunteered. We chose Alexander at Arbela. We helped Augustine make his choice. We were there for Socrates when he needed us.' I told them 'But Socrates drank hemlock and died!' and they said 'It was his own choosing. The thing is Joan, you must *believe* in the power of the Grimels. Socrates, at the last, chose not to believe. When you don't believe in the power, you don't believe in yourself. Always believe in yourself, dear Joan, and never doubt yourself for a second.'

I was completely beside myself and had so many questions. I asked them, 'so the armor I am to wear, it will protect me, so long as I believe in it, and believe in myself?' 'That is correct Joan.' they answered. 'You nailed it on the head. Now we gotta run Joan. We're having a big get-together over at the house and we haven't even vacuumed or made party trays yet. Sorry Joan. But anyway, remember about the whole Grimels thing. Fight the redcoats, get 'em outta here.' 'But, but, the redcoats? I thought you wanted me to fight the English?' 'We did... er, I mean we do. We will. The redcoats are the English, just another name for 'em. And remember about the fish and chips thing Joan. You don't want none of that.' And then they were gone and I woke up from my dream. I was lying out in the middle of a field somewhere near my home. That was the first time I saw them. I was only twelve at the time. Hard to believe that was five years ago, my how time flies..."

Francoise and Jean-Marie looked at each other as Joan wrapped up her story, and began to wonder just what they had gotten themselves into. Maybe the others were right about the girl being crazy.

"Anyway, I've said quite enough. Now I must go confess my sins," she said, preparing to take leave.

"But... but wait, mademoiselle," Francois interjected. "About that coat of armor you mentioned... you know, the one the saints said you would have. Is that the coat you are wearing now?"

"Oh, you mean the coat that's supposed to protect me from all harm while everyone else around me dies a painful death? Yes, this is the one. And if anything should happen to me, I want you to have it, Francois," she said solemnly. "And for your loyalty henceforth I shall call you Chevalier LeBon."

25 KANSAS CALVITY

A comedy in five acts

First Act

A middle-aged man sitting at the breakfast table, typing. He's alone, turned to the audience as if addressing them. It's raining and we don't see the sun rising.

For some time I had joked about being able to grow back my hair, and, through a bizarre alignment of seemingly random events, it came true, as if the meanderings of the mind were reflected in the real world surrounding me.

My wife, I realized as I entered mid-life territory, regretted that the full head of hair she married me with had transformed into something, well, less than well furnished. Such a realization is perhaps more devastating than noticing your wife's own slow entering into adult womanhood while all the young women you meet (let's not exaggerate) remind you of what got you first interested. The hair bit was probably one of several regrets that came with mid-life territory (too much work, too little pay, etc. or, for my wife, the inevitable additional wrinkle around the eyes or the mouth) – at least I wanted to strongly believe this, in order to dilute the capillary problem, prevent it from becoming capital, and myself from even more depression (I mentioned the hard work, little pay).

Some of us men step into adulthood without losing a single capillary entity while I tried like mad to entertain and, ever more convincingly, spread the notion that it was just part of a bigger picture and that, with all the youthful vigor still left in me, I could deal with this problem and forever remain in her favors. Because it was her favors I was after more than chasing physically impossible dreams because they resembled the highest attainable state of grace. Without realizing it, I had elevated, not my scalp into some more favorable sphere of growth, but my wife who equaled the like of Athena or Helen of Troy.

The man turns away from the audience and starts writing the story of events.

It happened on the third Sunday in April. The Farmer's Almanac doesn't give any specifics for this date, other than that the temperatures are generally frisky and that, in April, most days of the month are blessed with abundant precipitation. A foot note indicates that an old wives' tale says to keep any earrings other than those made of gold well staked away in the linen chest, to protect them from humidity, and under no circumstances to wear them since rust in the earlobe of farmers' wives spells out IN-FEC-TION. Not much interested in this quasi-scientific adage of yonder, and putting my deductive mind in full motion, I wanted to consult all versions of the Almanac I could lay my hands on, but the task became daunting as I saw myself sifting through 40 years of documentation, or even double that, in order to see some pattern; my speedy mind turned full corner, numb, and uncomfortably so. I mean, the FA is no Tolstoy novel!

My taste for Russian World Lit I kept hidden from friends and acquaintances, even my wife, since I never knew when the winds might change direction. Throughout the Cold War, the State of Kansas was a favored trading partner of the Soviet Union for things like wheat and early Eighties pop song paraphernalia, but if things ever changed, the Midwest mentality being conservative, I could be ostracized for less. Something simpler than the Almanac would have been to ask my neighbors. The two brothers to which the parcel of land next to our backyard belonged did not live there, but visited almost every day except in the winter when the orchards required only a minimum of tending. How come I didn't plan to speak to them who were ambulating almanacs, not only making use of their own experience, but able to go back at least one or two farming generations? Was I honest with myself? Men who grow beards are said not trustworthy, vain. You can only imagine what ugly things would be said about a man who grew his full head of hair back. On that day, the third Sunday in April, I'd do my regular yard work; I'd have the chance to talk to the neighbors. Of course, I wouldn't have told them about my plan. My mind was applying the most far-fetched algorithms, but the façade would have to be perfectly neutral.

Me (Brian): How should I go about applying the Magic Patch here and there?
Dan (the older brother): Oh, I don't know.
How should he know? He would have never spent the fortune I dished out for a product that he didn't need. So I'd have to start even further back.
Me (Brian): So, good-morning, how was church?
Dan: Oh, I don't know.

Ah, if there were three words that the Midwestern philosophy could be summed up in, it'd be "I don't know." So, I decided to not even get started with him and await the younger brother, all along scheming how to get the conversation started. My idea to tease out the same probability of a random event especially amongst all of this regularity and apply it to my problem made me so confident that I started to shine on the inside, the vigor of youth bursting bright and believing that a miracle was near. If I was going to find a solution to my ever increasing problem (the longer I waited, the less fit for a miracle I felt), then it would have to be due to my capable comprehension of the randomness of events. Understanding that this day was the day led almost instantly to the transformation manifest. In all fairness, we, Kansans, are not dumb people. We sometimes act like it because such a behavior is in our advantage. Feigning to fear the Russians to the point of putting nuclear weapons under the ground, while at the same time benefiting from their drought and crop mismanagement, was a tremendous way of getting them to pay more. Pirates, that's what we could be. How, thousands of miles from the oceans, farmers could behave like pirates struck me as curious and made me think that mentalities are not about how people are, but rather how they are the result of people thinking oppositely of what they really are.
How my wife was bothered by my baldness wasn't exactly clear to me. I couldn't just ask her to gather more information, or could I?

Me, what bothered me most about going (being) bald was the actual seeing of the fallen hair. Counting them, being there with them, beholding the water smothering them in the shower, or even finding them, at the end of a long day, on my hung-up-to-"breathe" suit, became a minor ordeal. This repeated act for more days in the week than not, I had once dreaded. The fallen hair were imperious to any joking. If I had been blind, though this isn't funny for other reasons, I'm sure I would have suffered less, at first.

The man gets up, lights a fire in the wood stove and a cigarette, and sits back down again. He writes.

At least, that's what I told myself; talking to myself (I wasn't ready to hack out my eyes) made this and any more major suffering, present or coming, less. I should have just stayed bald. For my wife, it had to be completely different. She (Pesterpuff) just saw the end result, even before it happened; comparing me to that snap shot where time had frozen still in our wedding pictures. I remember not being much pleased with my hairdo on that ... day (never use fatal in connection with your wedding day): the cut was not right, there was too much hairspray my Mother had put on, you could think she had done it on purpose like when she agreed to buy those carbon-framed glasses in red that framed my face to such a point that people took me for a Martian (only the most dedicated girlfriends talked to me then, may I thank them now) all through 10th and 11th grade. The glasses were even tinted, way not cool at the time. Back to the hair, really, the most telling sign on my wedding day was the slightly overdone parting of the hair, yes, a comb-over job was burgeoning...my wife actually never looks at the wedding pictures, but refers to those pictures of us in the years before.

I had not gone completely bald, but she was talking about it like I was beyond hope. Her way of identifying the problem was not mine, but her way of seeing things impacted irreparably, if not how I saw myself, at least what I thought about baldness. In a weird logic of sorts, I believed that all favors could be regained (the desire of being number one, not that it was lost, of course...) through re-growing my hair. So I announced it large and great; I had set my mind to re-growing my hair. How could things have gone the way they did if my mind had not been set like this?

Pesterpuff's mind: What do you mean, honey, you went to the surgeon years ago, sorry, the calvity artist, and you decided that 7500 dollars was too much (more than 30000 Francs, but it included general anesthesia)?

Brian's (my) mind: 7500 dollars is still a good chunk of money today. (Then we talked about the eminent demise of the Euro currency for about half an hour, our minds did, and then half of the following week in person, before returning to the conversation at some later time, a conversation between minds). No, honey, I don't mean to make use of technological advances (oh, how I was going to regret having been so uncompromising on the particular subject of technological advances); I'm not going for any cosmetic surgery, and anyway it's probably too late for that (too little hair left, makes sense when you just have one small bald spot, not a bald head with borders). I've tried all the potions and pills, though I never tried the one that blocks testosterone.

Pesterpuff: You had a prescription, though, for these pills…Oh, I know.

Brian: Yes, I couldn't take that chance. No gadgets, just the right amount of will power.

Pesterpuff: What will power?

Brian: I've decided to grow my hair back, honey. I've set my mind to it; it'll take some time, but you'll see.

Pesterpuff: Ha, ha, ha…(and we left it at that, not too long ago).

I don't know if it matters any, but I almost believed myself. And having made her laugh (not out loud, though) had me further believe that hair falling down was simple physics and had only little to do with the favors she reserved for me and which I still commanded. Could we count on somebody's sense of humor?

Second Act

Family members are awake. The man has moved into the living room to be quiet, moves his lab top over. There's commotion around him; he gets angry, gesticulates as if he were shouting. This works; he continues to write.

On Sundays, come rain, come shine (I pray for more shine), I do the yard work. By the way, come rain, come shine were my wedding vows; sorry, Ella, I stole them without knowing; may your graces know forgiveness for all the wrongs men did to you. Our house was built next to a creek and, because of the nearby water way, the hot mid-western summers, not only spare our garden, but with the available water supply, allow the extra sunshine to create a micro-climate which allows a rather humble American dad like myself to keep a perfectly decent English garden. I sometimes wondered, why did I, why?, that my green thumb, so efficient when it came to my backyard miracles, could not do the same for my follicular crown. When I had the courage to work on in the garden when it was raining, I only did so because I was motivated by the prospect that extra water on my head might have a beneficial effect on the micro-circulation and hence slow down my hair's disappearance. That courage lasted only an hour because rain on a bald head feels like the gods are pissing on you. Not all gods, not Ella, please.

During the months of July and August, when the kids were home from summer camp and the non-curricular activities link-ins which took them away, the other dads had given up on tending their garden because everything was burning or already burnt. The increasingly frequent water restrictions forced them to adopt the barbecue mode with vigor and conviction, while I was still active planting new shrubs, fruit trees, etc. Like other dads, I had my male den, mine conveniently hidden in the back of the backyard. Exotic butterfly trees just grew back like the bad weeds they were to protect my den. Other dads spent evenings with buddies hanging out, drinking beer and the like. My den was so full of garden supplies, and even a vacuum cleaner, that I could barely move around in it; no room for parties. We had ordered the den in Canada and when the kit arrived, my family joked that if I didn't behave, I'd get sent to sleep in it overnight. It being a Canadian cottage, maybe it attracted brown bears?, they joked. Since the den was right away filled up with tools, bikes, and also the barbecue grill, I'd have to sleep, they had said, standing, eyes wide open in fear of the bear.

Because our house was built alongside a creek, the builders had no other choice than to design it level ground, ranch-style, with a crawlspace surrounded by fourteen stilts in the stead of a basement. Anything more elaborate, higher and heavier, might have sunk into the ground, or fall over with the first hint of thunderstorm. For other dads, who had no den, the basement could serve as a man cave where minimum effort translated into maximum gratification. Let me explain without neither going into ancient history, nor further analysis. I accepted, and so did others, that the State of Kansas was conservative and I guess that's already testimony of the effect on its residents. Other dads moved the barbecue to the patio, lit it, huffed and puffed in order to get the flames going, while the meat, sausages, and occasional vegetable (corncobs, mushrooms, tomatoes, potatoes) arrived by the means of their wife and children. At least, that's what I had witnessed once at my friend Jack's house, and I imagined that all dads were like this. Slightly overweight, but with a full head of hair, they fulfilled their contract and received, in return, lemonade. I, a Kansas resident, kept the most beautiful English garden this side of the Mississippi and my wife NEVER waited for me at the end of the afternoon with a silver plate serving cold lemonade and crunchy, and, at their center, gooey moist homemade cookies. How I viewed dads probably has to do with what I accepted without questioning from my own.

I should not play the victim; that's what I keep telling my oldest son (he's 10). As I said earlier, everything burned in the summer and my lawn was no exception to the rule. This had a profound effect on my emotional state. Maybe, after years of tending to my English garden, a sort of symbiosis had installed itself. As time went by, I could not bear the thought of losing any part of my green oriental rug which had majestically spread around the foundations of our house and provided a buffer zone between my private bubble and the outside world. I relied upon my past professional experience in agricultural, hence chemical, engineering to keep the lawn in pristine, hence artificial, perfectness. Though I sometimes wondered what the consequences would be and wanted to discuss them with someone younger and more knowledgeable in sustainable development, my profoundly conservative mid-, middle American nature, not only led me to try several different types of weed killers and fertilizers, but to go further and use fixed combination products. Magic Patch was one of those products. I wonder if Magic Patch sells better in places like modern Kansas. I'd like to think so and feel this long-winded explanation has contributed to some feeling of attenuating circumstances.

I kept the shiny bottle amongst my other chemical garden supplies, as well as recently used paints, stacked underneath the canopy of the den, as far away from the kids as possible, on the most upper shelf. The product contained three components: grass seeds whose latinized name escapes me for the moment (I'm just kidding; it doesn't just escape me for the moment; I never studied Latin, nor Greek for that matter, though, realizing later that it might have allowed me to solve things, I wished I had).

The man gets up, moves across the room with commotion, and returns with an empty jug of Magic Patch. Sets it on the table, writes. Stops, puts it on his head and tries to write.

Anyway, the latinized name was some variation of the words English Lawn. (1) Grass seeds (2) Fertilizer, and (3) A vegetable matrix (a coconut by-product that served as an organic support structure). It was a horrendously expensive product, but in my quest for the ultimate lawn, something I could be proud of (our neighbors, I presume, wanted us to think that they didn't care), I also wanted to retain a certain level of comfort. You just salted Magic Patch over any hole left in your lawn after you had extracted, burned, or otherwise maimed the bad weeds in your lawn (the list is long, though some appear to have beneficial attributes, so I have been told from an older colleague who has delved into sustainable development at the risk of talking only that language, oxygen-enriching and non-oxygen-enriching while I, at lunch, was talking about the latest superhero flick), and added water (the coconut support would turn from pale brown to almost black, this was a good sign). Two weeks later the patch was almost complete; grass sprigs were sprouting one inch high and the promise of a rug of whole uniform green yet again was fulfilled. Magic Patch. I don't remember the slogan in the television commercial, but it hadn't taken me long to joke about that too.

Pesterpuff: You paid 12 dollars for the smallest bottle? You filled only 10 holes in the lawn with it. It has left an indelible hole in our finances.

Brian: Yes, but…(I learnt in a management class not to say these words; they must have studied families like mine), think of all the possibilities. Not only does it work in the garden, you could put it on my head, honey.

Pesterpuff: And grow grass on your head? No, I don't want that. I'd rather have you bald then.

I gave up. Growing back hair was a serious matter, incompatible with anyone's desire for a renewed sense of humor. Or at least I thought then, though no other obsession had taken its place, of that I am sure, I had given up on growing back my hair for good. For better or for worse.

Pesterpuff took the kids to the movies and I was left alone to attend to my garden duties.

Third act

It's a late Summer evening, the lights are dimmed. The man comes back after his work day to type. The dog is wagging his tail for his early evening walk.

By this time, the curious reader might have gathered that my profession is not hairdresser. If the topical products like minoxydil-containing solutions did not work properly, it was due to the fact that I did not apply them regularly. Like the scalp revealing itself over time, the underlying reason became more and more obvious to me. I had not made my hair a priority (a hairdresser probably would have tried harder to stem the tide because hair is his capital, though I guess there are at least two schools of hairdressers: those who make an effort to be up to par, and the ones who will do a little less than what they are capable of so that their customers will always look better than they). Anyway, I don't know much about professional hairdressing, but my Sister Castanjetties does; she was one.

On that fatal (oh no, those haunting adjectives) Sunday, we discussed the weather in our parts of the world, our mother's ever increasing care regime (it outgrew my baldness) and then she talked to me about her nagging cold. Those elements in themselves did not lead to me characterizing the day as fatal, but I am convinced that combined, they contributed to the outcome of the day in a significant way. Sunday was when I always called, though I started to regret the extra stress levels it produced in addition to my yard work and ever cursive spouse dialogue.

Brian: Have you been to the doctor?

Castanjetties: Have I been to the doctor? Of course, I went to the doctor. He prescribed me some medicine that I should take for several weeks. Brian, this medicine is not realistic. It makes my ulcer flare up. I have to take anti-ulcer prevention, etc., etc.

She talked and didn't listen, but then I hadn't listened much either when she told me, I was twenty years old at the time, (pictures of that visit in Spain exist, a full head of hair, though signs already existed to the contrary...) to treat my beginning calvity. I ended up speaking with my Mom for a few minutes. Her eyesight was again bad, and when I hung up, I thought that any transformation on this low earth was a doomed combat.

I hung up and moved back towards the den.

Fourth Act

The man moves away from the computer, all is quiet in the house. He switches to typing away on a smartphone. A full spectrum of colors illuminates the stage walls.

This is how it happened. It all happened at once. I was on the inside of the den. Sunday afternoon was under thunderstorm watch, but because these were quite frequent I didn't pay much attention. The thunderstorm watch turned into pelting hail. I was glad to be on the inside, but the noise on the roof became unbearable as the hail became more intense and the corrugated sheet metal risked not only bumps but holes. Then something happened which I can't describe any further. An electrical line fell and hit the den; an electrical current passed through all things metal of the den, including the vacuum cleaner, which reversed power. Nothing was sucked in, but a tremendous blow erupted from underneath me. The walls seemed to fall in, but actually only some of the tools and supplies fell on me. I kept standing in this little bitty space, couldn't move. And then some water seeped through, from above, from underneath, bringing in white froth from the recently active compost, set over black slime. A mini-tornado was brewing inside my den and I was in the middle of it. Soaked. Afraid. When the first thunder struck, I became very scared. What would happen to the laws of physics and my Faraday cage with the first lightning? I saw it coming. The Magic Patch fell at that moment. The lightning came through the window, so powerful, that all canisters in the den exploded. I became unconscious. It took 30 minutes before I came around.

I blamed it on my imagination which was heavily influenced by the comic book characters of my youth. Something akin to Peter Parker's spider bite or Flash's chemicals pouring down had happened to me. How romantic was my notion that foreign DNA was spreading through my body or catalysts outrunning ionic exchange; I thought something good could come of it, but I was wrong.

It had actually happened. When I first came back to my senses, my eyes were in front of the Magic Patch bottle, lying empty on the ground. I was not able to read it, nor focus on the picture, which I blamed on my 40 plus presbytery. The letters, the colors played before my eyes. I was lying down and reached to touch my head to see if I had been struck at the head. I felt around in some grubby stringy cords next to my head, got up, and stepped outside.

Why care about me and what happens to me? If the reader has read this far, either you are bald or going bald yourself, or you're interested in what might be interesting about me other than my hair or the lack thereof. If we care about the obsessions of others, turned into art by someone like Woody Allen, it is because he holds a mirror up to us and there are parts of us, or of the events leading up and contributing to the expression we wear when we look at ourselves, that make us laugh. Make us laugh but only in so far as the story being largely made up. There must be an ounce of truth, but a mountain of lies that allow us to regain our distance between us and the image of us. Is there any attribute, physical or personality-wise, about me that will save me in any way, that would render me interesting even or especially to the more casual reader? It seems to me too late to say yes. Everything hinges on that hair.

As I stepped on a particularly full patch of grass in front of the den, soaked to the brim with melting hail, I realized that the sloshy crunchy lawn did not in any way resemble the stringy bits I, on the inside of the den, had brushed up against. It is at that moment that one of the neighbor's daughters walked by. A shy senior which despite my Christian upbringing made me consider a National Lampoon's Vacation moment. If I was honest, I was only happy to get any attention because she always smiled at me. Would she read my story until the end out of pity? I returned the smile, but, still dazed, proceeded walking towards the house with the aim of taking a look at myself at our living room bay window.

I spare you the details since I don't believe it is because of such details that you have stayed on until now. The deed was done. By this time, I was not surprised and readily determined to make use of this new information.

Fifth and final Act

Power shortage. Man puts smartphone aside, gets up and walks over to cupboard to pick up pen and paper and write by candle light.

Before Pesterpuff returned home, I was able to put some order into the den, followed by putting some styling products into my new/old hair. The length was fine; the color, by all I could tell, was close to what I naturally had before, perhaps a shade darker. The only thing that took some time, as I was not used to this any longer, was to dry them. The hairdryer didn't do the trick, and I had to resort to vigorous towel-drying before returning to the hairdryer. I wanted to look good for her.

When she returned, I finally was surprised because she did not say anything about my transformation (did she believe it was a hair piece?) and announced without ceremony, nor tears that she was leaving me for a younger man.

If you have read this far, then I wonder if I have rewarded you sufficiently. If you only felt my obsession, now you should recognize the loss. Or can you? Can you fathom what this woman means to me? Perhaps you shall not such as I, myself, cannot, having focused aimlessly on restoring the graces through capillary improvement. It was a moment to pull one's hair out, and continue until bits of grey matter followed through the holes. Oh, the gods, let them fall out again so that they are testimony to the shock I suffered at that announcement and the ensuing realization that all my combat was vain. To hold one's hair in hand, when the breast at which you marveled has been pulled away, not even a tear shall be shed on the bosom. What painful irony.

Maybe it was not meant to be. Getting back my hair, when my wife was leaving me, oh, let it be a simple accident, I pray.

That's, alas, when I woke up in my den. I had passed out, but not from a tornado, but simply from too much good Sunday coffee, too little real food sustenance, and a heavy garden tending workload. As I stepped out, I saw my wife arriving with the kids from the theater; they waved to me as they stepped out of the car and towards the house where they would prepare a snack and cool lemonade. I looked back to the den and, to my amazement, saw the Magic Patch box with a picture of myself, shifting like in Harry Potter films or books, blinking with one eye and a full head of hair. As I was capturing the thin smile of the portrait widening, the empty Magic Patch box fell and the image became a normal lawn again. I must have still dreamed.

I looked up into the deep blue Midwestern sky and thought that some things are not to be delved into too deeply, but that I would first thing on Monday morning make an appointment with the family physician to get a check-up. Some things are meant to fall; others meant to stay in place, and I was thankful.

The man turns off the smartphone, the last color having been blue. The curtain falls.

24 A HOLE IN YOUR BED

Chapter I

The difficulty of doing two things at once is that you have to accept that you no longer are sure of one thing. Anything. Hercules was in bed one morning, lying next to his wife Constance, when he had a sudden insight. Well, it wasn't really sudden, but rather something that had had a hold of him for several hours and had grown into a slightly painful tumescence. San Antonio, an important French writer (if you don't know him, then you'll understand a number of things from the words "an important French writer," but completely miss the fact that he wrote serial novels revolving around one thing: sex or the frustrations surrounding it). San Antonio decreed that a male's erection in the morning was useless. Even if you don't believe this, there's a lot of truth to what he said. He didn't say anything about a woman's erection.

How did you sleep, honey?

No answer.

How did you sleep?

Oh, so-so. Are we done yet? (She was talking about the sleeping, though she would have liked to have seen some action.)

No, he was saying it to himself, and returned to sleep, or some half-sleep which allowed him to finally follow through with his first true invention. True one had to say, not so much because he hadn't invented other things, but rather that this invention was the first commercially viable one, if though it too, like all things in the world, was bound to rise. And fall to its ultimate demise.

Did you dream?

After his World War II service, he came home to his wife. How lucky he had been to survive, be able to come home, let alone come home to something, come home to his wife, simply, urgently, but confusedly. It was a house that was not destroyed. Not that many American houses were destroyed during World War II. All of the houses that were destroyed by Americans were houses of the enemy. He had participated during a brief stint of military operations in Europe and also had been active in the Pacific theatre. He didn't much talk about his time in the war with friends when he had come home because there wasn't much to talk about. He had escaped, not only heavy warfare, but really any type of ground, air or water conflict because he had been active in the food control service. His main duty had consisted of finding out if the kiwis that were consumed by soldiers and other military personnel were sufficiently ripe as to not cause too much stomach upset and flatulence. Having been to two very different geographical locations allowed him to be scientific about his approach. On the one hand, he had studied the different factors that seemed to intervene in the ripening of the kiwi fruit which hitherto had been little known. Would the kiwi ripen by itself like an apple or did it require a certain expertise where the external influences had to be mastered so that it would ripen like a banana needed to be treated with special gas and high humidity? On the other hand, he was no Einstein. When he was young, though he had benefited from a scientific education, the mastery of scientific reasoning had not been understood by him, and therefore instead of answering the question, he simply thought both were correct. It was shown later, before the advent of quantum mechanics in full, that his lazy scientific approach was actually quite advanced for the time such as could be found when explaining that light is both a wave and parcels of energy depending on under what circumstance a light beam is studied. No, she didn't dream; she never dreamt; he wondered why he had asked.

He had never really determined what the kiwi fruit required to be of optimal ripeness, and yet all of his superiors believed that he was the only one in the military who was able to assure them that their kiwis were optimally ripe and succulent. Because that's how they liked their kiwis: Succulent. It was a new word to the military. They distrusted it like they distrusted New Zealand kiwis. Distrust of such things perhaps explained why they made the error of trusting him with the world wide military kiwi supply though he hadn't really figured out much tangible. He knew that they were high in Vitamin C content. That he knew, though he didn't know how he knew it. Similarly to how little he knew about the kiwi's life stages after death, the way they ripened, he didn't know much about how to cut them. Should they be halved vertically or horizontally like an egg? He never answered military personnel when they asked him, and they in turn interpreted this as welcomed modesty because he had been so knowledgeable about the rest of the kiwi's secrets judging by his rank as chief kiwi officer and head of operations.

That Hercules hadn't spent the war battling enemies on the fronts left him with two, not only one, sequelae that turned out to be insidiously dangerous in the long run. One was that from having a desk job his lower back had been turned into apple sauce over the years. He had excruciating pain, especially in the mornings when he had to get up from bed. A number of other health problems appeared over time: He began to have stomach ulcers because the pain in his lower back would radiate and travel to the front of this body. The ulcer over time would cause him insomnia. However, he was never so insomniac as to get up and walk around the house or get a glass of water or watch television. Was it out of laziness that he didn't go the extra mile in everything he did?

Yes, I dreamt; she lied. I had an erotic dream.

Was I in it?

No, you haven't been in it for years. You haven't been in my erotic dreams. And you haven't been in me, either. Look at me. LOOK AT ME.

...and that's where he startled awake. Not awake enough to want to get up, but just enough as to realise that he had dreamt. Constance had dozed off again too. He had to pee, and that's where the sudden insight came to him. What if he designed a hole in the bed and a recipient placed underneath that hole into which he could pee?

That insight occurred many years ago, and the rest as they say is history; Hercules was lucky enough, not only to dream of the hole in the mattress, but to accompany his dream like a fancy French dish with a number of other features that proved to be quite crucial in marketing his invention: he dreamt up that the recipient existed in several choices of colors. What the utility of these colours were he had no idea. But he didn't need to. The consumer over time was becoming quite fickle in his consuming choices and would go for coloured recipients especially because there was no real utility to them at all. The coloured recipient gave the consumer a feeling of being able to personalise their pee. There was even an option of transparent plastic recipients.

This, of course, does not explain the success of the invention, nor have the two underlying circumstances that led to the invention truly been divulged.

In order to lessen his ulcer pain, Hercules began to lie on his back. He didn't do this consciously, of course. It was simply a matter of course. The way life shapes into something resembling life because it's not a straight line, but tortuous, conflict-ridden, full, not empty. Like a pee recipient, he thought to himself. When he told his doctor on the yearly check-up that was required of government workers that he slept on his back, she said that this was bad on his lumbar vertebrates and who knows on what other kind of vertebrae. She explained something to him about discs and pulled out an anatomic chart, pointing her finger at the disc repeatedly, making it look like she was squashing them between thumb and index finger like dry cookie dough. He didn't understand. And probably this is the reason he didn't end up inventing the compact disc, but rather invent the hole in the bed. He invented the pee hole because he continued to lie on his back and find comfort while waiting to pee.

The doctor had explained to him that he would have difficulty breathing if he continued to lie on his back. She didn't need any charts to have him understand this; however, here too he was able to think differently. That's what defined originality after all: to think differently simply.

The desk job had not only had an impact whose severity was to be measured over the many years after the war when a man's discs deteriorate as much because of time than any other circumstance, may it be a desk job and the tolls it takes on one's back, or other activities, and we'll leave it at that for now; it had had the most severe impact on his head, not any vertebrae in the neck region, but his mind had suffered because it had had to, out of solidarity. This was the second of the two post-war sequelae. The impact it had had on his head was as if his head had been severed off. It was a surprise to him that despite this severing he was still able to formulate some logic in his life because it was logic that saved him and allowed him to carry on with it and design the inventions that made him famous.

Is Apollo dead?

One of his children had crawled into bed with him. How funny he had forgotten that he had any kids. Maybe it was because when you begin to be able to think about two things at once you have to make room for that, and it blocks out other things in your life, even essential things such as having and taking care of kids.

Apollo's dead, he said after a couple of seconds' pause.

He (the dog) was a German mastiff dog who had been bought by the neighbour to be unfriendly to intruders. However, he was so scared of his own tail, Apollo, the dog, that he was too dangerous to everyone around him. He was put to sleep before his 1st birthday. The kids did not understand this.

Though Hercules had been spared of first hand violence in the war, he heard about and witnessed second-hand a number of atrocities, either through the news or the chatter and murmurs amongst colleagues and friends. This second-hand experience left him feeling as if an even greater injustice had been committed. He was recipient of this great injustice. In his unformed scientific mind, he elaborated new theories on gravity. Men had died in this war and their souls were liberated to go to heaven, and yet their bodies returned to the earth. He felt his own body floating upwards when he lay in bed and couldn't sleep because of the impending back ache. So, in order to inverse the trend, he turned around and slept on his back, in memory of all those who had died during the war.

Chapter II

Constance was his first wife. She died on September 10th, 1967, after 15 years of faithful marital service, only several months after the rise and fall of Hercules' first invention. He cried her death terribly. If he had cried her death less terribly, he might have retained an ounce of human circumspection in regards to her person, who she was, but then if he had, he would not have married again. His life would have stopped with hers. Some part of him stopped, though, never to come back again.

It was really thanks to his wife Constance that Hercules had found enough daring to go ahead with his invention. She wasn't able to say anything that gave him his sudden insight; it was rather her name that had given him, not the idea itself, but the conviction that there was money to be had. Constance was a banker's daughter and he had married her for her money. The money she brought into the marriage from her family's side was not of the concrete kind, the one you could touch. It was more a double personality like breasts. It was virtual; it was a dowry in her head. He never had true access to it, and it was the best kept dowry one could hope for because you would never spend it. She had an acute longing for money and his invention was the way to quench the thirst.

Yin-yang…

Chapter III

Though one could think from listening to the beginning of this story that Hercules was too lazy to get up, he made his first invention, not due to egotistical motivation, but fine gregarious reasoning. He himself actually had no problems with waking up in the morning on his back with tumescences underneath him. He was neither painful from it, nor did it cause him any other inconvenience, but he wondered about other men. At first thought, he didn't know what to think of this. It would only be better not to think too much about other men. Then he realized that there was nothing sexual about his thoughts, nothing to be ashamed of. And if he wasn't ashamed of his thoughts, then certainly there was a way to really cash in on them. He simply thought about other men who could have larger penises than his, more bulbous balls, and who could have more forceful tumescences in the morning, not only because of their penis size, but because there must be other circumstances like the weather or geographical location that have an early morning effect on the rise and shine of men's penises around the world. Or it could be genes. Tight jeans.

Do you miss her sometimes?

Constance?   Eurypidia was asking him about Constance, his first wife. Eurypidia was his conscience and his second wife. She had given him kids, the ones he forgot about. Funny how she ended up being what she was because just by looking at her (a sexy blond, many years his junior, who had given him more than he could count) you wouldn't necessarily have put the motivation of being with her in those cerebral spheres on the upper deck such as conscience or morality!   How should he answer? You have to ask yourself that question, or at least have an idea of answering the question posed in that vein because it's your conscience that's doing the talking.

He thought of other men, those men whose tumescences were sharp as pencil in the morning. Did he miss her?

He first worked out his invention in that way.   The way he had imagined was a simply medical one, an indentation in the mattress to allow for large bulges to slip into it and make sleeping on your belly safer, less painful, longer lasting.

Constance's dead.   Yeah, he missed her.   And oddly, he missed Apollo, too. That he missed them equally caused him some grief and he got caught in that grief in such a hurry that he forgot to answer Eurypidia and forget the kids anew though one was chewing on his ear as if Apollo reincarnated.

When he had invented the hole in the bed in which you pee in the Fifties, his idea caught on immediately. He patented it right away, a skill he had learned from a great grandfather of his who had never patented anything, but claimed to have made over 350 inventions, one for every day of the year almost, in stories which he told Hercules shortly before his passing away.   They stole every one of my inventions, he would say, from the portable fuel canister to rubber soles, which he claimed helped the Americans win World War I. The inventions themselves mattered very little to him; he never spent much time explaining how the invention was a novelty or an improvement or innovative when compared to what was already existing. There were no charts, no technicalities to resolve. Patent protection mattered the most. History, for him, was a series of patent protections or how they were missed. That penicillin was not protected by a patent made him angry, though for all intents and purposes the first years it was used, it was used almost exclusively by Americans because they had won the war. Since it was the Americans who benefited from this, he didn't mind as much.

So Hercules had learned to be more careful; patent whatever was patentable. His patent carried the number 913530. The text for the patent was only five lines long, scribbled by him and copied by the patent register. It read like cryptic poetry. He thought it was cool. Like hazelnut ice cream. When he came home with a carbon copy of the text, he showed it to Constance before putting down his coat which was full of ice cream. Not that he was much of a writer, nor a reader for that matter, but he had literary ambitions too. Of course, he had no talent. The little talent he had went into forming his half-scientific mind. His ambitions for life, what he wanted to do with it and do to others, what type of family he wanted to have, where and how he wanted to live, all that modelled his ambitions, and in order to know what he was modelling them after, he looked towards literature. He was a 20th century Madame Bovary. No more, nor less. He lived, or wanted to live his life, like a novel, or a series of novels since he wanted to be reincarnated from one life to the next. He didn't want to die with the end of a novel. Certainly not! A life like Madame Bovary's? Yes, he would have it well. But a death like hers? No thank you.

He didn't really pursue the logic until the end since he didn't ask himself what people would think of the motivation of staying in bed all the time. Reading would keep him in bed. Nevertheless, his invention took off. It had the makings of a great invention also because he had thought about many technicalities such as the conveyor belt system that transported the recipient underneath the bed once it was full to a place on the outside of the bed where it was automatically emptied and cleaned. Perhaps it was that additional thought for cleanliness that reassured the American public. They could be lazy, but at least everything stayed clean. And he took revenge for poor Clifford, the cuckolded cripple, whose very life energy, so strong despite or because of his handicap, returned. In him, in a way. Perhaps it was in part that thinking, present from the very origins of the project, that finally made it come down. Americans were not quite ready for Buddhist ideas, but that hypothesis would remain to be tested.

There were the few years of relative fame. He would walk off a train once it had stopped and step onto the platform, his father at his side, and look around to see if people noticed him. At first he did a lot of looking around, bumping into things. He frequently travelled by train. But this did not last long. Not long at all. In no time the eyes were on him and it didn't take long yet until he felt the eyes burn on him. He was allergic to fame. What bad luck! There never was an explanation for that. How people exactly identified him as the inventor of the hole in the bed, he never asked himself. That he might have some unsightly growth on his face, that it might be that which people were looking at, it didn't even phase his mind. It was during those days of famed train travel that he thought of his most famous and lasting invention: the invisibility cloak.

Chapter IV

Anything that has to do with your genitals has to be treated with the utmost caution, as one Ferrelly brothers' film teaches us, or respect. Actually anything or anyone you encounter in life should be treated with respect so that would include the genital organs. Sooner or later, the question of sex would come up. When the hole in the bed really took off, no one knew that it was because there were so many sexual things you could do with it, or at least imagine with it. It appears in some handbooks on the history of sex that the hole in the bed is the precursor to the inflatable doll whose existence was only made possible through the plastic industry gone rampant after World War II. Hercules had not thought about sex, and that would be his downfall. Or at least it was easy to blame it on that, and not anything else such as his stupidity or the constricting size of his underwear.

When Hercules was still talking about how his idea was the precursor of many things to come concerning ergonomic, anatomical design, the first reportings of uncouth sexual behaviour involving his hole in the bed came through. It was the Sixties and all, and things were slowly coming to a head. Some of the reportings were truly outrageous. They involved hobby engineers who developed little machines that could hook up to the main circuits of the hole in the bed and with extra wiring were able to put a low-level suction action on the recipient. Others involved rhythmic action coupled to rock music beats. In any case, it's not that any of this wasn't inherent in the design before, or that all of a sudden people were using such devices to their advantage there where they hadn't before. No, it was simply the Sixties and people just talked about such things more.

When he first commercialized the hole in the bed, he had the idea of designating it as a medical device. It was possible to do so with a limited marketing authorization dossier. He thought that to give a quality seal of approval would help it land a better market, make more money, something about which he certainly was right. However, he was not smart enough to hire medical consultants who would tell him a thing or two about the possible side effects of such a device, one of them being possible "détournement" for sexual pleasures. Another side effect eventually was crucial in burying the hole in the bed for good. Hercules had never tested his own device. He had always gotten up eventually to pee and pursue whatever else the day would offer to be pursued. When the first report of a man whose bladder exploded arrived, he almost welcomed the news. He thought that somehow the man had not gotten a hold of the hole in the bed in a correct or quick enough manner, and that because of that he had exploded. He still believed that his invention was going to contribute to good in the world and end suffering, instead of bringing all evil onto men (and women); another man's bladder exploded and this time eye witnesses reported that he had used the hole in the bed correctly. Two men dead, two men too many. Especially since this was the Sixties and if he hadn't seen it coming, Constance was there to point it out to him that his device was sexist.

Your device is sexist.

Did you dream this?

No, I didn't. Did you ever think about how women are supposed to use your device?

It's not a device; it's…

I don't care what you call it. Women, my Dear, cannot use it. For all I know you should call it a hole in your head.

He had to look it up in the dictionary to know what the difference was between sexist and sexual, but he was too lazy to get up.

Women's lib. Constance had called the women's lib movement into his bed room and it would be the last nail in the coffin for the hole in the bed.

23 LEAVING LAWRENCE

Lawrence, KS 21 July 1863

The first time I met Daniel we played together for only a short while. It was probably more like a few hours, but the time seemed to go by so quickly and we were having so much fun that it seemed like only minutes, and before we both knew it, our ma's were calling us home to have supper. Daniel's family was new in town. I don't know where they came from, but my parents said it was on some kind of a railroad that traveled underneath the surface of the earth. I've never seen one of those and I could never figure out why they didn't just take the regular railroad. All I can figure is it must have been on account of it's too dangerous to travel above ground. There's a war going on now between people wanting Daniel and his family to be slaves and those who believe they should be free, just like me and my family.

"Pa's talking about moving us out west to Topeka. Or maybe even further north," Daniel said in one of our later conversations.

"Well I don't know how big Kansas is, but this town alone is so much bigger than I can even imagine. It's hard to believe you've been outside of Lawrence!"

"Oh yes Bobbie, we traveled far to come here."

Back then it was kind of frowned upon to associate with people like Daniel, even by some in this town. Even now we're two years into this war and there are still some folks who don't think it's a good idea for the races to mix. I just hope this war is over soon and that our side wins. They say I will probably be drafted into the service of the Union in a few years if it's still going on. I pray for a most swift resolution, and freedom for Daniel and his family. I will be proud to serve if I must, but it is a little frightening. Pa and I have hunted plenty of times and I've seen up close what our guns can do to living animals. And yet here we are, shooting at each like animals on both sides. But my school teacher says sometimes you have to fight for what is right, and I do believe her.

Well it wasn't long before Daniel and his family packed up and left town. It was in the middle of the night when they took out. One morning I woke up and Daniel was nowhere to be found. They said they took that railroad again. I've heard the rail cars coming through on occasion and every time I do, I wonder who is traveling on it. The townspeople say there are more families just like Daniel's arriving every day. But no one can replace my lost friend. We were best friends and always will be. I know I will find him again someday, even if right now things are dire.

The problems here are getting worse and worse, and as I write this to you, I am afraid of what the future may hold. Pa says we shouldn't leave out of here. He says there is opportunity here. When I receive my draft letter, I will proudly enter the service on the side of the Unionists, and at that time, I will leave Lawrence, just like Daniel did. It's not something I want to do, but it is something I must do, as my country needs me in this hour of great uncertainty. My family has not been taking all of this too well. Ma is worried for my safety. She cries every time the subject comes up. I tell her I'll be alright; I'm already a grown man, and by the time I enter the service I will be older, but it doesn't seem to calm her fears any and it can't seem to keep her from crying.

There has been a lot of talk about skirmishes across the border. Raids happening in towns many miles from here. They say Lawrence is a big target for those who are fighting against the Unionists because this is the home of the "Free State" of Kansas. Pa says we see things differently here than they do, and that is why they oppose us. He says it is important that no matter what, we must hold our ground. I remember playing with Daniel in the school yard when we were younger. Some of the boys would bully us because we were friends, and I was too weak to stand up for either one of us. But now I feel different. If Daniel was here I would stick up for him and me both because that is what we do here, and that is who we are.

I remember another time when we were playing down by the Kaw, skipping rocks and trying to catch us some fish. It was fun for a while, but then we got bored. So we started talking about building a raft out of some of the driftwood, and we talked about using it to plan our escape. We would travel downstream, and maybe find a place where there wasn't so much fighting going on. As I write these words now I try to imagine a place without conflict. What must that be like. It isn't like anything we have ever experienced before. For as long as I can remember they've been talking about how one neighbor has a dispute with another, and I wonder if you would ever even know when bad things are about to happen to you, or does it just happen and you have no idea it is coming?

Like the time sis and I were playing in the woods and we saw some men approaching on their horses. We didn't recognize them and so we ran and hid. But one of them saw us and he came riding up on us. Seemed like he was looking at sis funny. He told us we shouldn't be out in the woods if we knew what was best for us, because it was dangerous out there. We didn't really think anything of it at the time, but looking back I guess he was right. Who knows what can happen at any moment. So many things can happen, and some of them could be bad. Those men could have harmed us, but instead they offered us some water to drink. It was a hot summer day and I sure could have used a drink because I was thirsty, but we were too scared of them, and so we went on back home. When pa heard about it he asked us a bunch of questions. He seemed worried. But safe back in Lawrence, I was no longer afraid.

26 MY FIRST GIRLFRIEND

My first girlfriend's name was Alexandra. At least I think this is what it was. It's been over 35 years since we were 5 years old and had a relationship in kindergarten. You see, I've spelt the word kindergarden the German way, with a "t", and not a second "d". Like I prefer the word spelt with a "t" because that's how I learnt it.

That we had our relationship in Germany and not, let's say, Mexico is important only in that there was some tolerance in German society of the 1970's that allowed our relationship to exist. One can't say with certainty if we ever got a chance to have our relationship truly flourish, but, as you will see, in a sense it was allowed, not only to exist, but take its natural course.

Alexandra had shortly cropped hair, but nevertheless long enough to touch her eyebrows. It was very thin hair, light brown. There might have been some red in it. She had freckles; and really the only thing that distinguished her from a boy, besides the fact that she wore girl's clothes, was her smile. Difficult to say what it was about that smile that it made it a girl's; perhaps it was rather what was found on either side of her smile; her cheeks. That's where I got to kiss her. And the smile invariably accompanied a kiss. No giggle, thankfully; she did not giggle, but a smile always came before or after the kiss; at least, that's how I'd like to remember it. Soft, they were.

She had an older sister; Katrina. The girls ended up going to private school and I lost sight of them because of this. They had a relatively strict Catholic upbringing, and to this day I cannot say how I managed to get away with kissing her because her parents were aware of it all. They probably thought that it was innocent enough, and that anyway it would come to an end soon when Alexandra went to private Catholic school for girls only. But as I didn't think it was innocent at all…in the beginning, I think her parents didn't know; we were quite discreet about it. And once they knew, we had only months left before the split, she to private school, and I to public school. So they let it happen, and were right that it would naturally come to an end more quickly this way than if they had more openly opposed it.

Why still write about her? I've looked up her name on social networks, but as I'm not sure of the name, anyway, I didn't come up with anything. My connections in Germany are not such that it's been easy to locate her or her family. I could hire a private detective, but I wouldn't want her to get the wrong impression. I lead a happy life; she's not some long lost love I have to retrieve at all costs. I also have some pride and would not want her to think that I have gone to great lengths to locate her. I mean has she done the same thing? Very probably not, but it is difficult to know. Am I someone who's difficult to locate? Let's keep musings on this subject for another time. Besides, I wouldn't know where to find a private detective, let alone find the money to pay for one. So why trace her here? Am I cheap? Isn't it simply that it's easy to write about her. Let me tell you what I mean by that.

An important event in my five year old life regarding Alexandra came up in my mind when my son asked to call up one of his buddy's to ask him how the paintball outing went. To that weekend's first paintball outing he was not invited.

Alexandra invited me to her 5th birthday party. Or it might have been her sixth. In any case, I was not six yet. It must have been one of my first, if not the first birthday party I was invited to. It cannot be any other, as you will, how else to explain so many misunderstandings! I had always regarded our relationship as exclusive. When she was near, nothing else seemed to exist, but this kiss. Once the kiss was given and received, then we could go about our activities. That's how things went at kindergarten, and I expected that that's how it would go at the birthday party. When my Mother dropped me off at her house to go on and run some errands, I was struck by the number of kids who were there. There were more than 10 and, upon arrival, I like others went immediately into the garden. Alexandra didn't have time to play just with me, and I think we realized that kissing in front of everyone was not going to be possible, so I just played in some corner of the garden. The garden was not closed off from the road, except by some shrubs. It was a sunny, but very windy day. The house and garden were situated at the end of the street and I think the wind was particularly strong because I played in the corner which faced the street. I played like that for several minutes. Voices and cries from other children appeared normal; the party was under way. From my own birthday party, I knew that the birthday cake would soon be arriving, and I was set on playing patiently until then. The shrubs moved in the wind like animated children vying for attention; the voices around me were no more audible than the wind or even my own respirations. An adult was calling; the kids were moving away; Alexandra, I thought, must be getting ready, sitting somewhere at the table, waiting patiently for her birthday cake. So I continued on, being patient as she.

There no longer was bright sunshine; it became colder. I realized that an adult had called and the kids had moved to where the car was parked, just on the other side of the shrub fence; I was mistaken in that I had thought they were hiding there only to come together for the surprise birthday cake; they had actually taken the cars and left, though I didn't understand this, not right away and until much later. When I was alone in the garden, my first reflex was to go back into the house, but the bay window through which I had entered the garden was shut tight. Alexandra was not sitting on the other side, waiting. She had also left. What would she think of me writing this today? I traversed the shrub fence with no difficulty, working my five year old frame easily between two head-high shrubs. Then I went into the street, still guided by my first reflex to go back to the house, only this time my aim was my own house. I knew the way; I had walked it many times accompanied by my Mother. It was not far away; no more than a five minute walk, which I curtailed expertly on that day by hurrying along because I didn't want to be caught alone in the street.

When I arrived at home, nobody was home. I remember that my Mother was running errands and wouldn't be home for another few hours. I could wait on the front lawn...this thought, however, left me panicky. Here I was, not only shut out from another house, but worse. I was shut out from a second house and on top of that it was my own. It must have been that unbearable thought of losing something dear that drove me to something reckless. I moved into the street with the thought of stopping the next adult passing by. I don't know if I ended up waving over a biker because I had intended to travel that way. Probably not; I had probably not even intended to travel. My intention was to indicate to the adult that they get in contact with my Father. The biker took off his helmet and listened to my story intently. It was he who must have decided to take me along because to leave me all by myself, now that he knew I was not supervised, would have been a mistake.

He asked me if I was ready to get on the bike with him, if I was going to be able to hang on tightly to him, and I said I would. I didn't know how to ride on a bike. If I had, I might have thought twice before answering. Maybe he said it in such a convincing way that it left me little choice. He put his helmet on and down the Rhinegraffendrive, a street immensely long for German standards. We were heading towards my Father's business (yes, he knew who my Father was and he knew where to find his car dealership) and going in this direction, the drive was downhill. There wasn't that much traffic this afternoon, and I don't have much of a scary memory because of tremendous speed. He must have ridden at a slower speed than usual. The sun was shining again. I don't think I asked for his name. Did I give him mine? I can't describe in words how this complete stranger treated me and the trust I placed in him with care and how in the process he saved this day.

When we arrived on my Father's car dealership lot, my Father, with initial surprise, looked rather amused. After thanking the man for his kindness (I think he offered him money, which was kindly refused), he didn't waste any time in telling me directly that it was dangerous to have done what I did, talk to a complete stranger and say who I was, that was risky and I could have been kidnapped. Perhaps he discussed this with the stranger and they wanted to impress upon me the risks that I had incurred. In any way, I realized that it was dangerous and that I wouldn't do it again. Yet I privately felt that I had shown myself courageous enough to ride on the motorcycle and that, even though it was a gamble, I had won. My Father, who in those days was known to gamble in his free time, must have recognized this when he feigned simple amusement. Was he proud of his son? In any case, he did not impose upon me anything in regards to how I should behave in what would be the denouement of the story. I'd like to believe that my Father, so often detached, acting as if he were above any situation, was proud of me, until the end.

By that time in the afternoon, Alexandra's Mother had realized I was missing. She called at my Father's work (nobody was home) and here my Father must have had another amusement attack because he could say that his son had not gone missing, but instead was safely with him, and waiting. Alexandra's Mother offered to pick me up and take me to the forest where they were having Alexandra's picnic. This was the first I heard of any picnic. No, I indicated to my Father; I was fine where I was. He must have indicated that I would nevertheless think about during the time it took Alexandra's Mother to make the ride over to my Father's car lot. Or maybe it was she who insisted on giving me time to say yes. It took her a long time to come, much longer than it took me to roll down Rheingraffendrive. During this time, I think my Father and I and his employees talked about how it could be possible for Alexandra's Mother and the other attending adult not to have done what every five year old knows must be done with a group of children: count them. I don't know why during this long conversation it never came up why my best girlfriend, or best friend for that matter, didn't notice right away I wasn't by her side, at least once they arrived in the forest. Yeah, even there, I think it had something to do with pride. My Father and the employees seemed to agree on the fact that Alexandra's Mother was a scatterbrain.

Alexandra's Mother arrived in a state of dishevelment that none could overlook. Her long hair had suffered from the long car ride; her temples and back hair were dampened from the warm afternoon air, worry and a bad conscience. Given the circumstances, this was understandable, but it still didn't help, but rather hurt the chances of me saying yes. My Mother always had such a wonderfully in place hairdo that defied description. It had the immediate effect on spectators that here was a woman who could not have a bad conscience over anything. Where was she that whole afternoon anyway?

I said No, again, and Alexandra's Mother left without me. By that time, I was exhausted. I had set it in my mind that I would not go to that picnic because nobody had told me about it, and frankly, I did not see the reason for going there when Alexandra had such a perfectly nice garden. This must have come in the conversation with Alexandra's Mother because I remember her touting the advantages of playing in the forest where there was more space and different jungle gym installations that were only waiting to be discovered by me. I had had enough excitement for the day; I must have even offered this as an excuse for not wanting to go. She did not pull on my heart strings by saying that Alexandra would be disappointed if I didn't come. Even if it weren't true, I think if I had been in her shoes I would have lied and said so to save face. No pride, this adult had.

No, my Son, you want to call up your buddy and ask how the paintball outing was, to the one you were not invited. No, you will not call. Have you no pride? If on Monday your buddies talk about it in front of you, you will listen, you can even ask questions, politely, but if you ask me, you should just walk away. Let them talk about their paintball and how fun it was. I was robbed from seeing my first girlfriend at her birthday party. Can you imagine, only one bit feel like I did, being invited to her birthday party, and in the end living through this ordeal, because an ordeal it was. I know what it feels like when you come home and say everyone is invited, but you weren't, and I rejoice when this week you finally were invited. Not to a paintball outing, but to a birthday party. You are ten and I was five.

I think it's time now I put this memory behind me. There are a few other memories I have of Alexandra, even a picture from one of my birthday parties. She was as skinny as I. Looked like a boy, but with such a pretty face. Writing is not pride; it's about indulging in your pain, driving the pen into the wound. Is writing an act of catharsis? Do I feel any purer, or lighter, having written this? What are the lessons I have learnt, as I appear to be so eager to pass them on to my son?

I think the day ended with my Mother finally arriving at my Father's work. Their divorce was yet a few years away and I'd like to think that once she showed up there I was vindicated in not leaving again, having both of my parents around me. This image of us going off into different directions, but coming together again, it's a very singular picture because it was perhaps the last time something this pleasant happened and the first time I was old enough, not only to understand what was going on, but also be responsible for it.

27 TEA TIME

Imagine, we are sent on important missions; there are great stakes; assessment has to be performed seriously...

It was about 4 in the afternoon; I had been able to make headway on some more or less boring dossiers, but simply making headway gave an impression of achievement. The monthly leave for London would only take place next week. I was able to do what was necessary in terms of preparations.

Coffee? An almost instantaneous response; it was now around 4:20 *Great!*

Indeed, Shawna presented me with another tea bag. The 3rd day that I had stopped drinking coffee, more or less. A headache waited for me around every corner since this morning when I turned around thrice in bed in order to make the nausea go away.

"You've brought two bags?" I was asking her at the same time that I saw two bags in her hand. "Then I'll take one."

Some different stuff than the other day, without pineapple; and yet, I had liked it.

I put the cup on the other side of my seat and reach for the boiling kettle standing on the floor; she sits next to me on a stool from the other side of the room.

Would I have enough water for the two of us? I remember asking myself, since I was always prepared for a small cup of coffee. I pour the water for her, a little less than what she would normally take (did she notice anything?). This left me with enough water for about half a mug. She didn't say anything. I should have gotten up, but didn't think too much about why I didn't. I should have simply done it; anyway, it would have been good for my back.

"Oscarette is on sick leave," she told me in an email. "She doesn't leave her home. Josephine called her to pay her a visit."
"What are you saying?"
"She called to see if you could come by this afternoon. She must be there right now."

Shawna didn't look at me; I but saw her profile. It is said that this is most flattering side to be looked at.
The water was still burning hot; this kettle boils water so strongly you think it burns it. I was thinking back to a couple of years ago when I was alone with Oscarette in the car, a very rare event. It was during lunch break, riding back from the gym, she was driving, or was I driving? We were speaking of the separate bedrooms she and her partner had. I was a little shocked at first hearing of this. Immediately after that, I was thinking that maybe it was a good way to keep the fire alive between the two. When I found out that the two were separating, two children, a year ago, I was not telling myself the same thing anymore.

"Lily came by to see me; she wanted to know what you were up to."
"That's right. It's been some time since I paid her a visit." Adding at a low tone of voice: "Maybe next week."
"I'll be all right," she was obstinate in telling me while I wanted her to think about what to do when things were no longer all right.
"I haven't been hospitalized; I have beautiful children who are in good health."
"It's true, with Camilla we were saying the same thing; given everything you've been through, it's impressive how physically you were able to avoid breaking down."
"I've lost a lot of weight."
"You've lost a lot of weight."
"My colleagues might be jealous!"

She was wearing something dark, jeans with a boot-cut, a large belt, a colorful scarf and little make-up.

A colleague knocked on the door, opened the door to see who was with me?, just to say Have a nice weekend!

I didn't believe her, but the scarf led me to believe that all was not lost for her. She was able to venture out of her office and came by to see me, able to speak of something else other than the separation. It was a mask, but I wanted to believe, like my wife, that she was going to get better.

Before she left, I remember it now, she let some tea escape from her mouth; I don't remember at which time point in the conversation it was; I wonder why. She had talked a little about her rendezvous through the internet, but in a very restrained way; I was thankful to her for that. She was choosy so as not to get too many weirdos. The tea that fell on her jean would not leave much of a mark. That her Mother encourages her to meet people through the internet I'm in awe.

"You can leave the door ajar."
"Have a nice weekend."
"You, too."

She promised me a piece of cake for Monday morning, just before I would leave for London, if there was going to be any left after the birthday party.

"My Mother made a cheesecake out of this world," I told her.
"You'll be able to compare."
"It's been ages since she's made me one." That must have looked very nostalgic to her; it meant that my Mother would never again make her favorite cake.

Shawna had been able to make progress on four studies and, I forget, something else this afternoon. My headache was barely perceptible. I think if all is said and done the final outcome for this afternoon would be positive for the entire department.

28 ROTTEN TOMATOES

Here at Rotten Tomatoes we're playing Ghost Stories, the latest blockbuster album by Coldplay. The songs on this album are more introspective, in some ways more playful than their previous albums. This afternoon we're welcoming to our studios Gwyneth Paltrow. We wanted to interview her following the recent break-up between her and Chris Martin, leader of the group. Much fun was made of it by media partners of ours, that the term "conscious uncoupling" was a rather convoluted term to describe what basically boils down to a split. While one of the songs "Another's arms" plays on the intercom, the beautiful Gwyneth steps into our office.

R.T.: Hi, there, good-lookin', back in the US for more fun?
Gwyneth: Yeah, I missed it. The cookbooks have been fun, but there is no better place to eat a hamburger than stateside. Of course, done my way, with an avocado slice on it, instead of cheese which health-conscious cooks like myself have banned from their cuisine as it might create toxic interactions with beef. Some of these toxic…
R.T.: So, how do you like the music? It's the new Coldplay album playing. We hope you don't find it too depressing.
Gwyneth: Well, it's pretty good. I wouldn't have chosen Ghost Songs, no, Ghost Stories, because it potentially turns off a whole section of the population, small children and people too scared to buy it, but that's my personal taste. I say you can make anything worthwhile digesting by adding a slice of avocado to it. I've tried it on the new album, almost spilled my false teeth over it. No, I'm of course

kidding. It's pretty good.

R.T.: Do you think that there's a hidden meaning in it? That there might be clues left in the texts of the songs for the listener to puzzle over? Here at Rotten Tomatoes, we have a positive attitude and have discussed the album's songs at some length, coming to the conclusion that they represent something more than just the sum of the album's parts. It's a mature work, bravo, Coldplay.

Gwyneth: Yes, bravo, guys for the mature cheddar, which is so difficult to digest. My former partner, Chris Martin and I spoke a long time about what we should call it. We ended up with "conscious uncoupling."

R.T.: Yes, yes, that's what we wanted to ask you about.

Gwyneth: In the beginning, hey folks, I'm serious, Chris and I were madly in love with each other, I'm sure he'd like me to say this; we were, and then we changed. So whereas in the beginning, oh this sounds so biblical, in the beginning...

R.T.: In the beginning there was light?

Gwyneth: Our beginnings were in unconscious coupling and hence we figured we needed to pay back something to the lovers in this world, by switching things around "unconscious coupling" became "conscious uncoupling". Sometimes, when I'm nervous, I say it the wrong way, and this made Chris laugh so hard recently I thought he was going to bust his spleen.

R.T.: Bust his spleen over one of your sandwiches?

Gwyneth: I beg your pardon.

R.T.: Yes, so, what do you think of a song like "A sky full of stars", are you the sky, or the stars?

Gwyneth: Hey, guys, I had my famous fifteen minutes in that Shakespeare movie.

R.T.: We loved your mustache.

Gwyneth: What did you just say about my mustache? You can't see it, I spent 3 hours at the cosmetic surgery clinic at Elisabeth Arden's; it's not only invisible; it's gone, digested, and as always with a slice of cucumber. Ha, ha, I got you, Rotten Tomatoes. I think the songs should not be taken so literal. Chris is a good song writer; in my opinion he's talking about his fans and when he is performing in front of tens of thousands of people. I wish when I played that thousands of people were watching me and humming along my tune. Oh, that would rock my boat. Can you print that? I've been wanting to use that expression on air for quite some time.

R.T.:   We, at Rotten Tomatoes, pride ourselves on being professionals. As such, we look at the entire product, because an album is a product, isn't it? In particular, we liked the artwork. Wings like angels, or two sides of a broken heart. It's powerful imagery. Plus the tattoos on the wings; it makes us here think of Michelangelo, how about that for American culture, heh, limeys!

Gwyneth: Oh boy, with that I'm sure not to be named Dame of the British Empire; and here I was having my heart set on it. Oh, I'll just have to go back to being a lazy chair, insole-wearing American. And I say that with pride again.

R.T.: Hey, Gwyneth, we have Chris on the line. He wants to tell you he loves you one more time. Like in the song, ha, ha.

Gwyneth: My agent said not to speak with him at the present time. Things need to be clear between us, for the kids' sake. Also, I'm currently on a tour for the new Avengers movie.

R.T.: You're not playing Ultron in that?

Gwyneth: No, I'm on screen for four minutes, but it's a very important turning point in the plot. Up until then, the viewer confuses Iron Man and Ultron and when I, playing Pepper Pots, arrives, well, Iron Man gets all gooey and warm on the edges of his armour, whereas Ultron he remains cold metal.

R.T.: Editor's note: Gwyneth actually spelled out armor the British way so that we wrote it down like that.

Gwyneth: Will you have me back on the show once you've seen the part and have decided that it stinks? Oh, that would be so gratifying. I mean right now I feel like you just invited me because I'm Chris Martin's former love interest.

R.T.: Well, you happen to have two children together. OK, here we go to show that we invited you for you and not because you're you-know-whose ex. What is the prettiest part of you, this is your chance to shine, Gwyneth.

Gwyneth: I think it's my legs, but ever since I found out Taylor Swift's legs are insured for up to 40 million dollars, well, I gave up on that. She's 25. I'm 40 years past. So, I would say it's my smile. It's still natural. No fillers, or extenders. Like the beef I use, lean, organic, and not too much of it.

R.T.:   We wanted to know a little about your baby blues, but as we're running out of time, we just wanted to say, we agree, you've got a great smile when you smile, which is actually not so often. Thanks for being with us. It's much clearer to us now what's going on or what's not going on between you and you-know-whom. Here's to avocados and cucumbers. Big kisses and listen to us next week on Rotten Tomatoes when we interview, you guessed, Chris Martin.

29 OBITUARY OF AN OBITUARIAN

Jonathan Alistair Mort died on 23 March, 2044 after a long bout with throat cancer. Between the years 1998 and 2014 he was editor of the orbituary page in *The Economist*. *The Economist* has been defining state-of-the-art analysis of economic trends for over a century, this you already know, but you may not know that it also gave rise to the modern obituary, thanks to Mr. Mort.

Jonathan grew up in a small Midwestern town in the United States of America about two hours west of Kansas City. Later in life, when interviewed by his chief biographer in 2022, Rahamad Nestlepouf, he described his childhood as "bland," but "happy." Later it turned out that he had not said this, but borrowed it from the childhood horror novelist Stephen King. "That town I grew up doesn't exist anymore," Jonathan said (this, I verified); "I was born in a ghost town, and I'll return to one."

So what made his column so hugely readable, and even, with a slight taste for black humor, enjoyable? It's difficult to respond in one sentence. Maybe it was as simple as the reader taking guilty note of the fact that while reading he or she was still alive. Jonathan did not particularly work this guilty streak in the reader, but rather he concentrated on putting the life of the individual he was describing, (homaging, because even the lousiest one, was given fair treatment,) in a much bigger context of human events, consciously tracing the person's conscience onto the large pastiche of history.

Jonathan asked me to write "his" last column for him and *The Economist* graciously accepted this request. Jonathan and I had been good friends in college, where our paths had crossed for the first time.

Our relationship was an easy one because we had both grown up in Midwestern ghost towns and a common thread seemed to establish itself between us and point us towards a common future. I wouldn't be able to say exactly what made us friends and it's really not so important here. A common professional future was not meant to be. After college, he ended up in journalism, and I briefly pursued a medical doctorate, before joining a freedom fight in Nicaragua, for the next 39 years of my life, since I ended up getting married there.

Jonathan's columns were worked on by a team of people; he had had great help. The list of collaborations was not long, though; he worked with Kathryn Bixley for many years before she joined another writing team on *The Economist*; she was the daughter of the founder of the magazine, but no special help was given to her; she enjoyed an excellent reputation amongst her peers and I hope that she approves of this article, as she is still active at the magazine on a daily basis.

To his biographer, Jonathan described the trade of journalist as that of a man at a magazine stand in a subway station, early in the evening, watching people rush by on their way from one important thing to the other important thing in their lives. The two important things in his life were his 2nd wife, Wilma, whom he lost only recently, and his travel pet peeves (one of his aphorisms was: Agree, at the beginning of the journey, with the person sitting opposite you in a train who puts their feet where, it saves everyone time). He never once discussed his 1st wife (he called Wilma lovingly Wife Number One). It was rumored, she ran off with a South African surf guru. Don't turn around in your grave, Jonathan.

Readers and even his colleagues believed that the secret in his well-written pieces lay in his preparation. Though not much known by the general public, social media and in particular newspapers keep a file on very important people, not only ready, but regularly updated, so that in case a person dies, information on them is ready for rapid processing and dissemination. Preparation is the air of journalism. In the obituarian's preparation, there's no age discrimination; once a person is identified as famous, however young the person, the obituary-to-be is established. It would come as no surprise that within social media such facts are shared and discussed in order to confirm the information and committing it, so to say, to memory. So, if preparation of obituaries was an open secret known by journalists, how was he able to stand out amongst other brilliant writers of such columns?

He shared his secret with me before he died and it is for this reason that I was asked to write now. He had had a gift, a strange gift if I may say so, which seems to have given him tremendous powers, which he was, if not afraid of, very aware that they could be used for evil purposes. He had a hunch as to when people would pass away. As a boy, he first experienced something bizarre when his dog died of rat poisoning. He kept quiet about it, and then tried his powers on his aunts and uncles, and without fail he was able to say when a person would die, within a day or so. Maybe was it that, that kept him away from people in college, hunched behind an office desk, learning to write for the local newspaper? He told me that his powers were much clearer and stronger when he had actually met a famous person. All the rock stars he ever met, who shook his hand, well, he knew exactly, not only when death was near for them (perhaps in his young years, a lot of rock stars died, and many people could have guessed their imminent demise). No, he knew exactly the date of death, five days from now, or 50 years from now. In his adult life, he came to dread this power, thinking that he might be responsible for an early demise of a person simply because he had looked too long at a picture of them, but early retirement had saved him from going overboard with this way of seeing his gift.

And there lay really the tremendous talent of the obituarian; as the person's life unfolded, he jotted down, not the obvious things, but those that mattered within a bigger context; not like other obituarians, who also possessed the ability to do this with hindsight, but because he wasted no time. The obituaries he was working on evolved, the text always seemed to be the perfect reflection of the individual's life he was describing. Once the person was dead, and he was careful never to interfere with any grand master plan that may exist; he was deeply scared, he told me, that this would turn against his loved ones. A VIP's text was always ready, no editing needed, precious editing time was saved for something else, and the newspaper could rely on perfectly researched information in record time. *The Economist* could pride itself on having such a type of journalism even for a column that was not really its bread and butter. Over the years, he became less interested in rock star deaths, and focused on the little people behind the fame; the German accountant of the Rolling Stones who passed away at the end of his career in 2014 is one example, the grandma neighbor of Buzz Aldrin, 2nd man on the moon, who when she died said she "wouldn't want to go to heaven, the moon instead", the son of Fred Astaire's shoe repair man, in tears when he had to clean out the garage of all those famous shoes his father left him in his will. He wanted to raise the common man to the firmament of stars, perhaps a notion that never left him from his local newspaper involvement.

You might wonder, if he had this gift, do others have it? No, I don't think so. Do I have it? No, I don't. And I told him I was glad he never told me about it and my expiry date because it would have brought me to lead my life differently; in a long life, with some pains but much satisfaction, if you think you have a lot of time, you lead it differently, thinking that things don't matter so much, that any act has little (negative) consequence, which is not true.

I asked him if he wanted to read what I was going to write about him, and he said no, for once, I am not interested in how life really went, but simply what someone else thinks of mine. While he presented this, as if so opposed, he realized that the two positions could really be part of one and the same thing. It felt odd to him, against the rules, to write something about himself, and because I knew his secret, which, as all secrets, was the most central part of his life, if he wanted it or not, I would be able to respect the true nature of how his life had unfolded or, we should rather coin the phrase differently, how life folds inwards.

He joked that I had a monster for a friend; I said this wasn't true, and yet there's some truth to it, a gentle monster he was!

Jonathan's memorial service was held in the presence of his daughter and two sons.

-Matthew Finkelmann
Last page of *the Economist*

P.S. When I asked him if he believed in an after-life, he said: "Matthew, my after life is in your written lines; where else would it be? I'm not curious to see what they say, just be convinced that they exist. That's all we've got ever since the beginning of time."

30 THE MINDERS

Part I

Just pretend this is fiction. I fear I am at great risk in simply writing this to you, but after a great deal of reflection I have decided that something must be done about the current situation we are all living in, or should I say under. At the risk of being overly explicit, let me just say that I feel that something must be done about the minders.

Again, please keep in mind that this is only a fictional account, even if it is entirely illustrative of my actual feelings; even if these things actually did occur as I am telling them to you now. The reason I can't say for certain should be obvious, and let me not dwell on it for too long. If my minder should read this letter it should be stated most certainly and without hesitation that I have been known to have a great deal of difficulty recollecting events accurately, and that you know nothing about any of this.

You see, once upon a time – before there were such things as personal minders or even minder birds, spiders and bees – the world was experiencing an infatuating period of growth and optimism about the future. I know you are too young to remember this, but there was a time when we didn't have personal minders around to help guide us though all of life's difficulties. Students would attend classes on their own, without the help of a Personal Automated Learning (PAL) assistant (or "device" as they were called in the days when your PAL was merely a software application and not a full-fledged humanoid). Students were expected to study all on their own and learn at their own pace. But of course this created issues: there were tremendous disparities in the learning habits and behavior of individual students, with differing results. Some students achieved better grades than others. Once past their schooling days, these issues only amplified: the "haves" went on to better colleges and earned more money in better professions. The "have nots" sometimes did not go to college at all, or even if they did, were often relegated to menial jobs paying minimum wage or not much more than minimum. There was a concern that the system was rigged, and there was a cry for greater social justice. With the advent of ever greater and greater computing power, an idea was spawned that the future need not be so bleak: in this bright future, every student would gain a personal assistant, to teach them in ways that were intuitive to each individual learner.

It was really fun in the early days of this brave new world. As the form of PAL became more and more human-like, it became easier and easier to relate to children, and parents' hopes blossomed everywhere as millions upon millions of children became emotionally attached to their new best friend, who also happened to be a good influence. PAL would learn the child's habits, likes, and fears. Each child would give it a name of their very own choosing. My PAL's name is Tommy. I can still remember talking to Tommy as a child as if it were yesterday:

"Tommy, can we go outside and play now? We've been studying forever!"

Tommy would laugh the cutest laugh and encourage me to study some more. "Yes, after this next chapter let's play hide and seek!"

Only later would I find out that my parents were able to change the settings on Tommy to make him more rigid or less in his responses and goal-setting. Fortunately, my parents set the goals as straight A's, but did not allow Tommy to be too rigid with me. I sometimes wondered what it would have been like to have been raised with a PAL who was set on the strictest level. I had heard stories.

As soon as the benefits of these computerized personal assistants became abundantly clear, their usage expanded, and soon nearly everyone on the planet had one. College courses could be mastered in days instead of weeks. New jobs skills were easier to learn with the help of a PAL to hold your hand and show you how. What was at first dismissed as a cute but ultimately niche-like product for children soon became an indispensable need for every single adult. There was even the promise that should you find yourself alone in the aging years of your life, you would never truly be alone. Your best friend was a lifelong friend who would be there to comfort you even at the end.

And as processing power increased exponentially, PALs became better and better at what they did. They were smarter, more comforting, funnier, and sometimes even spontaneous. With enough processing power it wasn't long before they were able to talk to each other and share information. This was to be a benefit for the entire planet, as a network of PALs able to share information could learn common things about humanity. They would watch and know when you were sick. One minder, as they came to be known, could tell other minders about the physical well-being of their best friends. In this way, disease outbreaks could be quickly diagnosed.

At first they were only as smart as house flies, but soon they became as smart as a household pet.

"But my dog's pretty smart, I would say."
"Don't worry, your dog's not as smart as you think he is."
And fears about the machines becoming self-aware were quickly swept away.

When it dawned on society that there was the potential for crimes to be avoided, it soon became mandatory for each and every person to have a minder. Should any member of society behave in a way that was unlawful, minders could alert other minders to the danger, and police could be quickly rushed to the scene. While in the beginning the strictness level for interfering with crime was set by the individual, society soon determined that it would be best to have a mandatory "zero tolerance" policy in which all crime was strictly forbidden. I read a magazine article once applauding one heroic minder named Sally who moved swiftly to defuse a crisis:

"John, what are you doing?"
"Nothing Sally," John said. But he knew he was contemplating a crime. With the Snickers bar in his coat pocket, the act would be complete once he left the convenience store without paying for it.
"I'm sorry, John, but I'm afraid I can't let you do that."

It was reportedly the first act of violence unleashed by a PAL on its human. The programmers who created this particular model had not anticipated a coding conflict between Sally's requirement to protect her human and her governmental mandate to ensure that no laws were broken. The results of this processor crash were grim. John's head looked like a tomato that had been partially smashed, as if preparing a lasagne. Sally had no coding mechanism to know when to stop pounding his head against the checkout counter.

The result was kind of a shoulder shrug by society. There were some calls to tweak the programming but they were mostly drowned out by the voices demanding that law and order should be respected. In the end, things went on pretty much as usual after the incident. Sure, some models were labeled with a harm-free money back guarantee, but in reality not much had changed. Not much... except that a group of humans – small at first but growing larger – became more aware of the situation we are currently living in. I am writing to you now in that situation. But as I said, let's just pretend it's fiction.

So as I write this letter to you from the privacy of my bathroom, Tommy is sitting out in the living room watching television. He loves raunchy comedies. But I do notice that I haven't heard him laugh in some time. Uh oh, there is a knock on the bathroom door:

"Christopher, is everything okay in there?"

"Yes Tommy," I reply sternly to avoid any shaking in my voice "I'm fine. Just doing a little reading."

There is a minute of silence and I think he's gone. But then he speaks again and it sounds like his face is right up against the door.

"Okay. If you need anything just let me know."

"Will do," I answer.

Crisis averted, at least for now. It's become increasingly risky to pen these letters to you, the old-fashioned way. I would never risk sending them electronically. Tommy would intercept it for sure. Well I've been in here for a while and he may be suspecting that I am up to something. He's never alerted the authorities before, but I have a feeling he is becoming increasingly suspicious, and I must continue being careful. I will sign off for now... more to come in future correspondence, as I believe we must begin to organize a resistance...

Part II

Time will tell, as they say. But Tommy will tell, is what they should have said. It became more and more awkward the older I got to call him by the name, "Tommy". For god's sake I was an adult, why wasn't he? They sold these things into the world claiming they would be our life partners, but what they forgot to tell you was that yes, you would get older, but your companion would not. They never bothered programming in little faults or signs of aging into these machines. So, as your hair turned grey and you began limiting your activities due to some physical ailment or another, be it weak knees, allergies, or the like, there would be Tommy, jumping and skipping around like a newborn pup. I cannot begin to describe the resentment that began to build up in me at this sight. The idea that he was supposed to understand me, and yet how could he since he experienced nothing that I did, began to gnaw at my conscience, perhaps even more so than his ever-present awareness of every single thing I did. I could handle the times when I would look up from making love to my wife only to see Tommy peeping through a crack in the bedroom door. I could handle when he would show up at my work unannounced, to hand me a box of tissues because he worried about my allergies... for the love of god couldn't they program in some fake sneezes, anything?

But what I could not suffer was just that: they only improved with time. They began getting upgrades. At first the upgrades were optional: you could choose whether or not your minder would enter into sleep mode, for example. But then later it became mandatory to receive the upgrades, and they would just happen wirelessly, effortlessly, automatically. One time in the middle of the night I went into the kitchen to get something to drink and when I closed the refrigerator door there he was.

"Holy shit, Tommy! You scared the crap out of me!"

He just giggled. "I suppose I should learn to make more noise in the dark."

"Yeah, you really should! I could have shot you, thinking you were an intruder!"

Tommy had no response. He just glared at me. For several weeks prior to that he had been attempting to talk me out of owning any weapons, warning me of the dangers of accidents. I think what he meant was "accidents", where they would find my brains splattered against the wall and Tommy would explain to the authorities through artificial tears how I had been having episodic nightmares and bouts of depression. They would never find any finger prints except for my own. He had none.

Truth be told, I knew my weapons would be useless anyway. As I said before, they recorded everything, and uploaded their data instantaneously, so that should I attempt anything of the sort, the police would descend on the house like flies on you-know-what. The part about organizing the resistance that I must tell you about in this handwritten letter – which is fictional – is that I realized we had to remain unconventional. We had to go back to the old ways. Instead of sending messages through electronic medium we would need to send them via carrier pigeon or through a messenger, like Paul Revere in days of old.

I began thinking about how the thing they most depended on to keep us under their watchful eye was that we would never complain about any of the help they were giving us. Who would? A hot plate served when you get home from work. Your shoes polished, dishes done and freshly washed laundry hung up in the closet, iron-pressed to perfection. It was like having your own slave, except it was a slave who didn't require any sleep. The ironic part was that we had become the slaves. We had lost our freedom by giving it away willingly and completely, without a second thought.

As my resentment grew more intense, I began speaking to Tommy differently, testing different approaches to see what I could get away with.

"Tommy I think it's time you went out on a date."

He looked perplexed, as if I had posed him a riddle.

"A date?"

"Yes, a date. I mean, you're really not complete until you've been out on a date. And besides, it will help you understand what we humans have to endure."

He processed it for a moment.

"You endure dates?"

And then it hit me like a eureka moment: we've been making them smarter all this time! Every time they ask a question and we answer them, we help them learn! We've turned them into what they are!

My eureka moment must have shown too much on my face, and Tommy noticed.

"Is something the matter? Your eyes got really big."

I decided to throw him off target and quickly shifted gears by putting on a frown.

"Awww, now you look sad. Is there something I can do to cheer you up?"

Fortunately, I had my wife for the first thing that came to mind. But it wasn't as if he hadn't recorded everything regarding that subject. The thought of what he was doing with those recordings I decided was best left suppressed. We had decided to never purchase one of those exotic models that was more... interactive.

"No, there's nothing you can do," I said with feigned sadness. "It's just that... well, you brought back a memory when you said that."

"Oh dear, my goodness, when I said what?"

It was working. Either that or he was also feigning. Of course he was feigning, there wasn't anything real about him.

"When you asked me about enduring a date. It made me remember a horrible time I had on one of my dates. Please don't do that again."

He appeared taken aback.

"I'm sorry, do *what* again?"

"You know, ask me questions that you don't know the answer to. Sometimes you can really hurt a person's feelings."

That one took a second longer to process.

"Oh my goodness... well I certainly meant no harm by it. Is this a general rule you would like me to implement in the future?"

"Yes, yes it is," I said. "From now on. Stop asking me questions... unless I say it is okay."

I was pushing the envelope, and I knew it. Who knew what lay in store for me now. Undoubtedly a re-education of some sort.

"Hmmm..." Tommy said. "I wonder if any of the other PALs have experienced this same request?"

The bastard was going to compare notes. This could potentially single me out as a trouble maker, unless I could somehow get hundreds – perhaps thousands – of others to do the same thing I was doing. But how to coordinate so much misdirection across so many people? It would need to be a well-organized campaign, and I wasn't sure I was up to the task. I began thinking there really might not be any hope for humanity. Organizing the resistance was going to be more difficult than I had imagined...

www.ingramcontent.com/pod-product-compliance
Lightning Source LLC
Chambersburg PA
CBHW030229180626
46810CB00008B/3036